The Christmas Kiss

and Other Stories

Elizabeth Woodcraft

Ladder Press

PRAISE FOR ELIZABETH WOODCRAFT

A Sense of Occasion, the Chelmsford Stories

'Woodcraft's take on growing up mod in Chelmsford is poignant, heart-warming and hip.' **Val Wilmer, author of *Mama Said There'd Be Days Like This*.**

'Woodcraft's Chelmsford stories are intense, easy, evocative of times, places and passions.' **Beatrix Campbell, writer and social commentator.**

'A lovely, lovely read.' **Tommy Steele**

The Saturday Girls

'Beautifully written ... she has a real talent' **Mary Gibson, author of *The Bermondsey Bookshop***

'A book to read in great gulps' **Sheila Newberry, author of *The Nursemaid's Secret***

The Girls from Greenway

'Her genuine love of the era shines through in this beautifully written saga which brims with the spirit of youth and is rich in period detail.' **Lancashire Post**

'It's a fabulous read.' **Tony Fisher, BBC Essex Radio**

~ ~ 0 ~ ~

Good Bad Woman

'... sparklingly written, with believable dialogue and a lively plot.' **Marcel Berlins, the Guardian**

'My current favourite is debut author Elizabeth Woodcraft ... funny, engaging.' **The Bookseller**

'She has a record collection worthy of any of the characters from High Fidelity.' **Evening Herald, Dublin**

'Sharp, streetwise and engaging.' **Western Mail**

'.. unusual and compelling ... with the bonus of a Motown soundtrack.' **Time Out**

'Frankie Richmond is a great creation - more please.' **Cath Staincliffe, Manchester Evening News**

'Good Bad Woman is an unchained medley of love, loss, laughter and the law.' **Val McDermid**

Babyface

'Elizabeth Woodcraft has created in Richmond the sort of lawyer that we want to side with, ... in touch, switched on and with a life. Move over Rumpole.' **The Times**

'Witty and well-plotted this is a funny, action-packed legal thriller.' **Birmingham Sunday Mercury**

'The plot clever and racy ... Richmond is lively and self-deprecatingly funny, and the frenetic, unreal atmosphere of the bar is portrayed with authenticity and wit.' **Marcel Berlin, The Guardian**

Published by Ladder Press in 2022

Cover Design Christine Wilkinson

Copyright © Elizabeth Woodcraft

Christmas at Schmidt's was first published by Ladder Press in
2020
The Christmas Kiss, short story, was first published by
Ladder Press in 2021
The Traffic Jam Christmas, The Christmas Cracker and The
Christmas Play, were broadcast
on BBC Essex Radio on 24 December 2021

ISBN 978-0-9929208-6-9

For the newcomers, Rudi, Rafi, Thomas, Robyn,
Sunny, Mavi, Kyle and Harvey

Contents

Christmas at Schmidt's

Two days before Christmas Marie went to London to do some last-minute Christmas shopping. She had the day planned out. The train to Liverpool Street, then the underground, to Oxford Circus, some shopping in C&A and maybe Marshall and Snelgrove, dinner in Littlewoods, pick up a last few bits and bobs, then back to Chelmsford.

She'd arranged this day with Bill, her fiancé. He was coming too. He would buy a new suit and after dinner in Littlewoods they'd look at the lights in Oxford Street, and then maybe go for a Christmas drink, have a glass of port, be silly, like old times before they were engaged, before they started saving up to get married. It was going to be such fun, the two of them in London together, bickering over what to buy their mums, the colour of his suit, what they thought of the lights, but then at the last minute he'd said he couldn't get the time off work. He'd rung her from a phone box at eight o'clock this morning, his voice echoing as he explained the problem, it was a new job and this new boss was very strict about rotas. She was sure she heard someone giggling in the background, but he said it was traffic. She couldn't say any more because she was so disappointed that he wasn't coming she thought she might cry and Bill hated it when she cried.

Now she was standing on her own, on the platform at the station, her leather coat buttoned to the neck against the biting wind, waiting for the fast train to Liverpool Street. Someone tapped her on the shoulder. For a glorious moment she thought it was Bill, saying he'd wangled it with his boss and got the time off after all.

She turned, her face beaming. But it wasn't Bill. It was Johnny. Johnny. She hadn't seen him for months, ever since he'd stopped working in the greengrocers over the road. That was the week before she got engaged to Bill. Someone said Johnny had gone to work on the boats, to be a purser on the Dover to Calais ferries.

She stared at him now, scarcely able to believe her eyes. He looked tired and older, she thought, wrapped up in a camel coat with a scarf wrapped round his neck.

'What are you doing here?' she whispered, as if he'd come deliberately to confuse her, as if Bill had arranged for him to be here, as a sort of test of her loyalty. 'I didn't see you in the shop. Are you back working in the shop?' There was hope in her voice.

'No, I'm back up to the Smoke. I'm going home.'

Her heart dropped a little, so home was no longer Chelmsford for him. But she couldn't deny the warm glow of pleasure she felt, just seeing him here, so close to her. 'What have you been doing in Chelmsford then?'

'Tidying up a few odds and ends. There's nothing there for me now, just a few old oranges and that brown overall. The Hayfield Estate is finished for me.' He flicked a glance at her left hand, where almost on cue the small diamond slipped round her finger. The ring was too big, it had been too big from the start but Bill said it would be too expensive to have it made smaller. 'What about you?' he asked. 'You running away from home?'

'Ha ha,' she said. 'I'm going Christmas shopping.'

'Oh yeah? What have you got to buy?'

'Presents.'

'What you getting Bill?' he asked. 'A small bottle of arsenic, by any chance?'

'Not this year,' she said.

He laughed. She felt slightly breathless. She remembered the teasing, how she had loved the teasing.

The train puffed into the station. Johnny looked at her with a raised eyebrow. 'Shall we?' He opened the door and stood back.

She climbed into the train and he followed. Her heart was beating fast. Johnny, Johnny.

They walked along the narrow corridor until she found an empty carriage. 'Which side do you want to sit?' he asked. 'Don't tell me, I know. You hate sitting with your back to the train.'

'It makes me sick.'

'I remember.' He laughed. He sat down opposite her and rubbed his hands together. 'This is nice. We'll have the carriage all to ourselves till London.' He watched her unbutton her coat. 'I remember that dress too. I always liked it.'

You only saw me in it once, she thought, smoothing the skirt over her knees.

They sat in silence for a while. She looked out of the window at the bare fields, the skeletons of the trees. Her stomach was churning. Why did this have to happen now? She'd made her decision. The ring on her finger said that.

The ticket collector pushed open the door of the compartment. She fumbled to find her ticket in her purse. Johnny chatted easily, asking the man about his day, how many passengers, any trouble? what was the worst day to work? The man seemed pleased to talk, not so busy at the moment, he said, but Saturdays were the worst, the football fans, cheerful or miserable, they all ended up drunk. At last she found her ticket. He clipped it efficiently and then wished them both a very Happy Christmas. He heaved the door across and they were alone again.

'I thought he was going to tell you his life story!' Marie said.

'I thought you'd got on the train without a ticket. I was softening him up.'

She laughed.

They were passing through Ilford station, nearly at Liverpool Street.

'Where are you going at dinner-time?' he said, almost casually.

'Dinner-time? I don't know. I haven't thought about it.' She wanted to see what he'd say.

'Fancy having dinner with me? If that's allowed.'

'Of course it's allowed,' she snapped. 'I'm not under his thumb. I can do what I like.'

He smiled. 'All right, keep your hair on. There's a place I go sometimes. It's near Oxford Street. We could go there. It's called Schmidt's.'

'What?'

'Schmidt's. It's German.'

'What do they eat in Germany?'

'I'm not all that sure, but they do some nice things in the restaurant.'

'A restaurant!' She wasn't dressed for a restaurant.

'Yeah, but it's really casual. And the Germans like Christmas, so it should be good.'

'I don't even know what *you* do in London, let alone the

Germans. I thought you worked on the boats.'

'I did that for a couple of months, but to tell you the truth, I'm not a very good sailor. I spent more time heaving than working. So now I'm with a record company.'

'You're not!'

'I am.'

'Which record company?'

'Decca.'

She'd heard of Decca. They had a lot of records with that word DECCA spinning round and round on the turntable. 'So, what, now you know the Rolling Stones? the Bachelors? Dave Berry?' This wasn't fair.

'No, I don't do any of that. I'm mainly involved in the classical side.'

'You!'

'Yeah, me and Beethoven, we're very close.'

'Ha ha. Well, I know you can't sing, so what do you actually do?'

'Deliveries, and I do sing. In the van. A lot of opera.'

'You don't.'

'No, I don't.' The train was slowing down. 'Give us a bit of paper and I'll write down the name of the place.' He looked at her distraught face. 'And I'll give you instructions, how to get there.'

They walked through the ticket barrier together and he came with her to the entrance to the Central Line. 'See you at one, then,' he said and bobbed down and kissed her quickly on the mouth.

She gasped. 'Maybe.'

'One o'clock, upstairs in Schmidt's.'

'All right.' She entered the Underground station, wondering what she had agreed to.

She stumbled a little as she went up the stairs. She knew she was late, she'd been so careful, but she'd got lost, she didn't know if he'd still be here, and she wasn't even sure now if this was the right place, she didn't know why she was here, it was a mistake, she shouldn't have come.

The large room was crammed full of people sitting at small square tables and the conversation was loud. There was a strong smell of cabbage, and damp wool. A large Father Christmas hung on one of the nicotine-cream walls, beside some haphazard paper chains and pictures of cities, decorated with tinsel. The tables all had white tablecloths, a few with Christmas wrapping paper where people were cooing over gifts, laughing, having a good time.

Waiters moved round the room carrying trays, looking surly, occasionally tripping over coats and scarves trailing over the backs of chairs, but skilfully maintaining their balance.

She looked desperately round the room. She couldn't see him. He wasn't here. She was too late. This was awful.

She turned to go. The disappointment in her heart was heavy. And her shame at how disappointed she was.

And then he was there, behind her, as she put her foot on the first step down.

'Where've you been?' he said. 'I tried to save our table, but we've got to share it.'

She was cross with him for being so cheerful when she had been on the verge of tears. 'Well, let's not stay then,' she said.

'No, no, you'll like it. Come on.' He led her to a table in the far corner of the room. A man stood up as they approached.

'This is Marie,' Johnny said proudly. 'The one I was telling you about.'

'Johnny!' Talking as if they were a couple.

The man held out his hand.

'You look like Billy Fury,' Marie said, taking his hand. He had the flicked back quiff, and the slight sneer as he smiled.

'Do I? Well, you can call me Ronnie.'

'He *is* Billy Fury!' Johnny laughed.

Marie flushed with embarrassment.

A waiter came and pulled out a chair for her to sit down. 'There's a table for you now,' he murmured to Billy Fury.

'Well, folks, lovely to meet you. Have a good Christmas. And a good life.'

'Thanks.' Johnny grinned. 'Same to you.'

Marie watched Billy Fury move across the floor and greet a woman with dark eyes and a fur coat. They kissed lightly and he ruffled her hair. Marie was envious of their obvious happiness at being together, their relaxed, public happiness.

'Don't say I don't show you a good time.' Johnny was looking at them too. 'They all come in here. You know, pop people, people from the BBC. But it turns out Billy Fury's got a contract with our lot.'

'Well, it was cheaper than having to go to a show, I suppose,' she said, putting her carrier bags carefully on the floor.

'If we sit here long enough, we might see Elvis Presley,' Johnny said.

'Pigs might fly,' she said crisply, but she was pleased he'd remembered she liked Elvis. And wouldn't it be a laugh if he did! That would be something to tell Bill. But she wouldn't be able to tell Bill. She wouldn't be able to tell anyone. What she was doing was forbidden. Being engaged to someone and being with someone else, someone she wanted to sit very close to, to kiss, to whisper sweet nothings to, it was wrong. It was probably a sin. She had had to choose between them and she had made her choice. That's what the ring said. Johnny could never have afforded this ring. Was that what had done it? The fact Bill could afford nice things?

The waiter loomed over them and Johnny looked at her. 'What do you fancy?'

She didn't understand.

'To eat.'

She shook her head.

'How about some sausage and mash?'

'Is that what you're having?'

'Yes.'

'It is potato salat,' the waiter said.

'Salad?' Marie said. She looked up at the waiter's face. He raised his eyebrows slightly, daring her to challenge him. 'All right.'

'And two beers.'

The waiter nodded grimly. He picked up her scarf from the floor and tucked it over the back of her chair, then slid away.

'Good morning?' Johnny said. He was wearing a different sweater she noticed. It was navy blue. It suited him. He must have gone home to change. She wondered where home was. 'Buy all your presents?' he was saying. He had to repeat it.

'Yes.' She was suddenly reluctant to talk - about her morning or anything at all. She didn't know what she was doing here. She had done her shopping in a dream, mechanically looking at soap and gloves and toys, distractedly paying with notes and coins and receiving change. She'd looked at her watch repeatedly. She couldn't wait for 1 o'clock when she would see him again. His face, his voice, his laugh, were with her all morning, even his smell, the faint smell of soap, Imperial Leather or maybe shaving cream.

And then coming here, to a foreign restaurant, where everyone seemed to have a German accent, and where in the shop below she'd seen and smelled strange cheeses and meats and other things on display that she couldn't even describe. And after all that, bumping in to Billy Fury, as if he was someone who lived at the end of the street, someone you recognised but only to say hello to. Billy Fury who sang 'Halfway to Paradise'.

'I got something for you,' Johnny said, and put a small square box on the table in front of her.

She looked at the box and then up at Johnny. 'What is it?' she whispered.

The waiter appeared with their food, the potatoes glistening with oil and flecks of green. He banged down two bottles of beer and two tumblers. Five seconds later he was back with knives and forks and paper napkins. The box sat in the middle and she couldn't take her eyes off it.

'Leave it till after,' Johnny said, tucking his serviette into the neck of his sweater. 'What do you think of the sausage?'

She rolled her eyes at him and he laughed. 'Go on, you'll like it.'

She sliced through the tough, tan skin and speared the pink meat onto her fork.

'Have some potato with it.'

She shovelled on the potato salad and put it in her mouth. It all tasted different, sharp, unnatural. She wasn't sure she could swallow. She forced herself. Then she laid down her knife and fork neatly on the plate. 'I'm not hungry,' she murmured.

He poured some beer into a glass. 'Have a drink,' he said.

She sipped the beer. She didn't even like beer. Why hadn't he remembered that? She toyed with the glass, running her finger up the side.

He pushed his plate to one side. 'I'm not hungry myself.' He looked at her. 'Oh god, you don't like beer, do you? I just remembered. That time in the Red Beret, and I bought you a pint, so proud of myself that I'd got you a drink before you arrived. And I just assumed you'd like beer. I hadn't realised you weren't that kind of a girl.'

She smiled. It was their first date. She and Bill had broken up again and she'd been under the weather ever since, even though it was always her who did the chucking. Her mum said if she was going to have the day off work, she could at least do the shopping. She'd gone into the greengrocers and he'd served her. There'd been some confusion over the oranges and they'd bumped noses. He'd laughed. 'Fancy going out for a drink?' he'd said. 'Just to make sure we don't have concussion. Half past six in the Clock House?'

'If you like,' she said, casually.

She'd made an effort to look nice, had a bath and washed her hair. She'd even worn the dress she'd been saving for the dinner dance she and Bill were meant to go to. She had to say she was going out with her friend Deirdre to a works' do, because her mum and dad were hoping she'd get back with Bill and they didn't approve of Johnny from the greengrocers with his jeans and his greased back hair.

In the Clock House she'd looked for him, but like today, she couldn't see him. Then she noticed him at the bar, laughing with some of his pals. She felt foolish, all dolled up in this stiff, shiny dress, and all the hair lacquer she'd put on. But when he saw her, his eyes widened with pleasure and he said cheerio to his friends. He picked up two glasses, both foaming pints of beer, and came over to her. They sat in a dark corner and he'd put one of the glasses in front of her.

She'd looked at the beer and looked up at him. 'What's this?' she'd laughed. 'I don't like beer.'

'Oh god.' He smacked his forehead with his hand. 'That was meant to be a thoughtful gesture. What do you want?'

Now he knew her and he said, 'I don't think Schmidt's run to rum and black.'

'I don't drink that any more,' she said.

He frowned. 'But you love it.'

'Yeah, but I go a bit mad on rum and black.'

'Oh, let's see if they've got some tucked away somewhere. Waiter!' he called.

'Stop it!' she said. 'Can I open the box?'

'I don't know,' he said. 'Perhaps it was stupid.' He put his hand over it.

'It's Christmas. It's just a Christmas present, isn't it?'

He sighed. 'Of course.' He pushed it towards her.

It was a square pink box tied up with black ribbon. She undid the bow, looking up at him, and then she took off the lid. It was a necklace, a fine gold necklace, with a sort of pendant. Carefully she lifted it out of the box, and the chain slipped round her fingers. There was an inscription, in delicate curved letters.

To Marie from Johnny with all my love

'That was quick!' she said. 'When did you get that done? Or did you buy it for someone else?'

'Of course I didn't buy it for someone else. How many people do I know called Marie?'

'I don't know. You could have met someone. Some singer at your Decca place, Marie Antoinette or someone.'

'I bought it months ago.'

'What do you mean? For me? Why didn't you give it to me?' It was so lovely. She would have fallen head over heels if he'd given it to her then.

'I was going to give it to you that night.'

The night Bill had come back with the ring and begged her forgiveness, the night her mum and dad were so happy. The night she'd ended it with Johnny.

'You should have said!' she cried. 'You should have said you'd got something for me.'

'Now she tells me!' He threw his hands up. 'Well, are you going to put it on?'

It was so beautiful and so delicate and she was never going to be able to wear it. 'I can't,' she whispered.

'Just for the afternoon,' he said. 'I can't take it back. I told you – I don't know anyone else called Marie.'

'All right,' she said, and he stood up and came round behind her, so close that she could smell his sharp fresh smell, and he took the necklace from her hands and put it round her neck. His fingers brushed her skin as he fastened the clasp. Then he stood for a moment, his hands lightly on her shoulders, before he leaned down, and whispered in her ear, so close that it tickled and hurt, and he breathed, 'Do you want to go to the flicks?' and she said immediately, 'Yes, yes I do.'

He signalled to the waiter, put a five-pound note on the table and they left.

They hurried down Charlotte Street, their heads bent against the biting wind. There was a swirl of snow in the air as they walked into Rathbone Place and down to Oxford Street. 'What do you want to see?' he asked.

'I don't care.'

They walked along Oxford Street to the Academy. He bought two tickets to a film. 'It started 20 minutes ago,' said the young woman in the kiosk.

'That's how I like your films,' he said. 'Then I have a good excuse for not understanding a word.'

Marie stood watching, touching the thin gold pendant, playing it round the chain.

Silently they made their way down the stairs into a dark auditorium. She could make out the silhouettes of 5 people, dotted throughout the room. On the screen a man and a woman were talking to each other in black and white, squinting in the sunshine. Marie and Johnny walked up to the back of the room. She stumbled on the steps and he held her arm. They slid along the row and eased themselves quietly on to two, soft, plump seats. She pulled off her coat and realised she'd left her scarf in the restaurant.

She turned to tell him and he leaned towards her, his face cold from the outside, his eyes glittering in the darkness, like she remembered them glittering, sitting in the back row of the Regent in Chelmsford. 'What?' he whispered.

'What?' she murmured and he leaned in closer and she lifted her face to him, his smell, his breath, his mouth and then they were kissing.

Kissing and kissing, his hand holding her neck, and then his hands began moving over her body, her breasts, holding them, pressing into them, and then down, down to her skirt, easing it up towards the top of her stockings. She knew she should stop him. This was too much. This shouldn't happen. Bill did none of this. Ever. Even when the house was empty and they could do anything they liked. Bill respected her, he said.

Johnny's hand was on her bare thigh now. She was breathless with desire and excitement. Johnny, Johnny. But she had to stop him. She crushed her hand down on to his.

He nuzzled her neck. 'Sure?'

'Yes.'

'It was worth a try.'

'Easy for you to say.'

He laughed and kissed her ear then sat back in his seat, but he kept his arm round her, playing with her hair. The couple on the screen were walking through a forest now, looking tired and sweaty.

Marie wondered what would have happened five months ago, when they went to the pictures in Chelmsford, if he'd tried it then, would she have said yes, go on? And if it had gone on, and on, later, in his van? And if she'd got pregnant? Would she have married him then? Would she have sent Bill away? Would she have been happy for the rest of her life?

She closed her eyes, tears pricking at her lashes. He was looking at her.

'Hey!' he whispered. 'Hey!'

She shook her head.

'You haven't had anything to eat,' he said. 'You're hungry.'

She looked up at him, and said, 'Is that the problem?'

'We could go over to Littlewoods and have egg and chips.'

She put her coat on and they crept out, laughing a little.

In the glaring fluorescent lights of the Littlewoods canteen, she shook tomato sauce on to her chips.

'So are you going to marry him?'

She shrugged. "I suppose so. My mum and dad will kill me if I don't.'

'You don't want to marry me?'

'It's a bit late now.'

He was silent for a moment. 'I want to take you home,' he said.

'I want you to take me home,' she said sadly.

'No, you don't.'

'I do, but I don't. I can't.'

'So you are going to marry him.'

She raised her eyes slowly.

'We could still see each other,' he said.

'How?' she said wearily. 'How?'

'Eat your egg and when you've got more strength, I'll tell you.'

She laughed, but finished her plate, mopping up the last of the egg yolk with a piece of bread and butter.

He pushed the plates to the end of the table.

She put sugar in her tea, and a spoonful in his. Is this what married life would be like, she wondered. Knowing how much sugar someone took? 'So, you had some ideas how we could see each other.' There was a silence. She laughed and shook her head.

'OK. How about this?' he said. 'You get a job in London, and sometimes you have to stay over, and you could come and stay with me.'

'A job in London.' That sounded far too exotic. Bill would think she'd gone mad. What job could she get anyway?

'Like a hotel receptionist, or something.' He'd almost read her thoughts. 'You're so pretty, they'd love to have you on the front desk.'

'He wants us to live in the country. I'd have to come in to Chelmsford to get the train up to London. I'd never be able to get to work on time. It's going to be hard enough getting him to let me have a job at all. He wants us to have a baby really soon.' Johnny looked at her sadly.

They both lifted their cups and drank.

'OK,' Johnny said, 'but he's got to let you come to town to do your shopping, hasn't he? You could come up, I dunno, once a month or something? Haven't you got friends up here that you need to come and see?'

'I never come to London.'

'You never come to London! Hello, Earth to Marie. You're in London now.'

'Yes, but this is a special occasion. I haven't been to London for years. It would be funny if I started now.'

'Don't you want to see me?'

She paused. 'I don't want to live a life full of guilt.'

'But if you didn't see me, would it be a life worth living? Don't you want to have fun? Don't you want to go the pictures and walk out half-way?'

'We walked *in* half-way.'

'There you are, walking in, walking out, double the fun!'

'Oh Johnny.' She put her cup carefully back in the saucer. 'Look, I don't know anything about you. We went out once? Twice?'

'Three times,' he said. 'Four if you count that time you and your pal bumped into me in the Prince of Orange.'

'But that was Chelmsford. You live in London now. I don't even know whereabouts. You meet different people. You eat different food, potato *salat* and those sausages. For all I know, we're too different to even get on.'

'But we can try. We can make a start. You liked it when we saw each other.'

She remembered his kisses, his arms round her, laughing. How she'd felt this morning when she saw him on the station platform. Pleasure.

A woman in a gingham apron came and took away their cups. Marie looked at her watch. 'It's late. They're closing up. I've got to go.'

'Shall I come to Liverpool Street with you?'

'No,' she said. 'No, don't come. It'll be too hard.'

'Oh Marie. Look -' He snatched a paper napkin from the dispenser at the end of the table. 'Have you got something to write with?'

She took a pen from her bag.

'This is where I live.' He was writing. 'And this is my phone number.' He handed her the napkin. 'It's true what I said on the necklace, Marie. You have all my love.'

'Don't start!' She looked up at the ceiling. 'I can't keep crying.' She fumbled with the clasp of the necklace, and put it in her bag. She stood up and put on her coat. 'Bye Johnny,' she said. 'You stay here, while I go.' She left the napkin on the table and walked out of the store.

She hunched into her coat against the wind, struggling through the cheerful crowd of last-minute shoppers. The glittering Christmas lights swayed across the street, the shops were bright with fairy lights and tinsel. Her mind was churning. Bill would ask where her scarf was. He'd given it to her for her birthday. She'd never liked it. She squeezed her eyes shut tight. There'd be a row. Her mum and dad would join in. This was awful. And it had been such a lovely day.

And then, Johnny was there beside her. 'You forgot this,' he said. He crushed the napkin into her hand, then turned and walked away. She watched him, then carefully put the flimsy piece of paper into the zipped pocket in her bag, took a deep breath and walked down the steps into the Underground.

The Christmas Magician

Marvo, the Magic Santa was in his sparkling grotto in Bonds. All day breathless, excited children formed a queue. As each one stood before him, Marvo magically pulled a small Christmas gift from behind their ear. So many children. By the time Holly arrived, there was nothing left. They looked at each other, stricken.

'Wasn't I magic enough?' Holly whispered. A tear rolled down her cheek.

'Of course you were, darling,' he said, beckoning to his elf. From the back room the elf fetched Marvo's magic wand. 'Take this,' he said. 'I saved it for the most magic person. You!'

The Christmas Party

The activity room had been decorated for the season. The Christmas tree in the bay of the large room winked and glittered. The paper chains, looped across the ceiling, waved gently. There were three walking frames, two wheelchairs and six walking sticks, all carefully stowed at the side of the room. The other seven residents, carefully holding the wooden rails along the corridor walls, had arrived under their own steam.

Hilary and Vivienne, the activities workers, had chosen a Burl Ives LP of Christmas songs. The room was filled with his cheerful gravelly voice singing 'Santa Claus is Coming to Town'. Hilary rolled in a trolley with a tea urn and plates of biscuits. Vivienne handed out cups.

Each resident was given a Christmas cracker that parted easily in the middle, and there was muted cracking and wailing as small gifts flew across the room.

'Hats on, everybody,' said Hilary.

The choir was late. Hilary asked one or two people

if they wanted to dance and then she and Vivienne did a clumsy jive in the middle of the circle. 'Why don't you do the twist?' called Doris.

'Wrong music,' Hilary shouted back breathlessly.

Charles arrived as they collapsed laughing in the alcove by the window. He hadn't been too well since the day before yesterday and he really hadn't wanted to come, but Anitra, his special carer, said that everyone would miss him and they all wanted to see him. He didn't believe a word of it, but he knew Anitra tried hard. And it was Christmas. So he put on his best brown cardigan that zipped up, with his tan trousers, and he asked Anitra to dig out his brown brogues. Wearing slippers to a Christmas party was unthinkable.

He eased himself down into the only spare armchair. 'You look very smart,' said the woman next to him. He turned. It was Doris. She lived in a room on the corridor at right angles to his own. He didn't know her particularly well, and indeed he had always been slightly wary of her, ever since he heard her arguing with Vivienne about what constituted a decent afternoon's entertainment, and how bagpipes were not worthy of the name musical instrument.

'I could say the same for you.' He nodded towards her paper crown. 'It goes with your eyes.'

She laughed. 'Cheeky! It's red.'

'Oh no, purple,' he said, confused.

She touched his arm. 'Just kidding. Where's yours?'

'I think I missed the boat.'

'Hilary!' Doris called. 'We need another cracker.' She turned back to Charles. 'Quick, before the choir gets here, I'll tell you my joke.' She smoothed out the small square of paper from her cracker. She squinted at the words. 'No!' she said. 'Can't read it, and these are the wrong glasses.'

'You could borrow mine,' he said, pulling his glasses case from his pocket.

'Thank you.' She balanced the new glasses on the end of her nose, on top of her own. 'Ah, right! Well, it's not that good. I hope you weren't expecting a hilarious joke.'

Charles, who had not been expecting anything, said, 'Mildly amusing will do.'

'All right. "Why do bees hum?"' she read.

'I don't know.'

'Because they don't know the words.'

'Oh yes, very good.' He smiled. 'It's the way you tell them.'

'I bet you say that to all the girls.'

'I used to be a theatrical agent, so yes, I did.'

She drew her head back and looked at him. Then took off the extra pair of glasses and looked again. She handed the glasses back to Charles. 'That's very exciting.'

'Not really. I didn't get the Vivien Leighs, or the Greer Garsons. I handled the second spear bearers and the understudies' understudies.'

'Someone's got to do it.'

'I suppose so.'

The choir was arriving, bringing in cold air from the outside, and loud apologies and laughter for their late arrival. Hastily they arranged themselves in three rows, and throwing cheerful red tartan scarves round their necks, began singing Once in Royal David's City.

Charles and Doris sat quietly watching.

'They're not very good, are they?' Doris murmured.

'Well, they're trying.'

'I always wanted to go on the stage,' she said.

'What stopped you?'

'What do you think? Children, the war, a husband who would have died rather than see me wearing greasepaint. Well, he has died now, but I was too late to try the greasepaint.'

'That's a shame. You have a certain presence, you could have done well.'

She laughed. 'That's very kind of you. I think you may be confusing the size of my backside with my artistic abilities.'

He laughed too. 'How would I know? My eyes haven't left your face since I sat down.' He stopped abruptly. He'd meant to be gallant, but it had sounded as if he was flirting. He couldn't think of a worse impression. Flirting was not something he did. Barbara, the woman in the room next to his, was a flirt, trying to get friendly with the man who delivered the vegetables to the kitchen, calling out to him as he passed by her window. Everyone knew; even the staff were talking about it. Flirting was embarrassing.

But Doris was calmly eating her digestive biscuit, brushing crumbs from her lap. 'You don't often come to these Dos, do you?'

'No.' He considered his answer. 'There's something about the very thought of them that makes me feel old.'

She looked at him again, drawing her head back to get a better view. 'But you are old,' she said.

'It's very kind of you to say,' he said.

She nudged him in the ribs so he almost spilled his tea. 'You know what I mean. We're all old. But that's good. You know why?'

'Why?'

'You can get away with murder.'

'Get away with murder?' he repeated. 'What do you mean?'

'We can do anything or say anything.' She stretched her legs in front of her. He noticed that she too was wearing outdoor shoes, neat black leather lace-ups. 'Either people don't even notice us, or they think we're going soft in the head.'

'Do you want to get away with murder?'

'Sometimes.'

'Well, I'm glad your husband's not around, or I might

think you want me to knock him off.' He stopped. Had he been disrespectful?

She cackled. 'No, I just want you to look on the bright side. You have a habit of looking like a wet weekend.'

'Do I?' Had she noticed him? He sighed. 'You're right. I am a bit of a misery at times.'

'Oh, you're all right.'

Hilary was walking across the room towards them.

'Watch out,' Doris said, 'fun and laughter on the way.'

Hilary gave Charles a cracker. 'Shall I pull it with you?' she said.

'No thanks, Doris and I will do the necessary.'

'And very nice too,' Hilary said, smiling in a way that rather irritated him. She walked back to the choir.

Charles and Doris pulled the cracker. He felt surprisingly cheerful. He was enjoying talking to her. He unfolded the green paper crown and put it on his head. Doris adjusted it, so that the gold stripe sat to the side, at a jaunty angle. 'What's your joke?' she said.

He put his glasses on. 'What did the hat say to the tie?'

'I know this one,' she said. 'You hang around and I'll go on ahead.'

'Very good,' he said.

The choir were packing their things together, and calling goodbye.

'Why are you here?' Doris said suddenly.

'Oh! I'm sorry.' He looked round the room. 'Were you saving the seat?' With embarrassment, Charles struggled to his feet. 'You should have said...' He was surprised how sorry he really did feel.

'Silly sod, sit down!' Doris tugged his arm. 'I didn't mean *now*, I'm quite happy sitting here with you. You're the most interesting person I've talked to in months.' She paused theatrically. 'Well, you laughed at my joke.'

'I wouldn't say laughed exactly.'

'That's what I mean. But my question was, why are you here, in the Beeches, in Chelmsford?'

He sat down. The corners of his mouth were raised in a smile of relief.

He told her about running the agency with Gwen – she was always the people person – but then she fell ill and died, and after that he'd rather let things go and his daughter Marion had half-heartedly offered to have him at her house in Galleywood and he'd hoped it might work but he'd overheard her talking on the phone to her husband Richard and it was clear they were having problems and he didn't want to make it worse. So here he was. Marion lived five minutes' drive away.

'But she doesn't come to see you, does she?' Doris said.

'You're a very blunt speaker, aren't you?' Charles shook his head. 'She's young, she's got the children. We never got on that well. I – I wasn't at home much.'

'She didn't know her luck,' Doris said, putting her cup and saucer on the floor and slowly sitting back up. 'Cyril – my husband – was around too much of the time. Couldn't hold down a decent job. Bashed me about a bit, in front of the kids. No kid should see that. So, I *might* have asked you to do him in, but obviously, you wouldn't have wanted me to do Gwen in. So it couldn't have worked. It had to be – what's the word – reciprocal.'

'Like Strangers on a Train, you mean?'

'I loved that film. I sat through it twice the first time I went to see it. I came out feeling a lot better, as if there was a way out for me and the kids, if he went too far. I just had to find the right person for the job. But then Cyril went out one night and never came back. They found him lying in the paddling pool in the rec, dead drunk. Well, dead, actually.' She sighed.

'So all your prayers were answered.'

'I wouldn't say that exactly. He left me with a load of debts, rent, the never-never man, even a chimney sweep came round one day for ten quid Cyril owed him.' She sighed, looking into the distance. 'I worked like a dog that year. But yes, that Christmas was the best we'd had, everyone laughing and joking and making as much noise as they wanted.'

The music had changed. Charles recognised a cha-cha-cha rhythm. He tapped his foot.

'Do you dance?' Doris said.

'I'm sorry?'

'It's the tea dance now.'

'Oh dear.' Immediately he regretted the comment. Why did he always sound like a misery? 'I haven't danced for years,' he said.

'Come on then. Put your cup down.'

The last time he'd danced was – what 1957? Some dinner-and-dance do that one of the Grade brothers had put on. A place near the Palladium. Full of theatricals. Gwen had worn a fancy blue raw silk dress, and he'd dug out the dinner jacket. There had been a lot of sherry and beer and he remembered how red his cheeks had felt all night. They had spent most of the evening on the dance floor. The waltz was his favourite, but the foxtrot, the cha cha, even the tango, were all part of their repertoire. Bumped into Tommy Trinder at one point. Gwen was very dismissive of him as a comedian and now as a dancer. 'Clumsy clot,' she said. Val Parnell stepped in, in the Ladies' Excuse Me and afterwards Gwen had said Charles must talk to him, make some contacts, suggest some names. Everyone was smoking enormous cigars.

'Are you coming?' Doris was beside him, her hands on her hips.

He rose from his seat. The memory had left him winded with pain but he forced a smile. 'Ready, willing and able.'

They walked onto the space left by the choir. How easily his arms slipped into place, how pleasant her hand felt lightly on his shoulder, and holding his hand and then they were dancing. The music washed over him and his feet followed.

'Well, you're a dark horse,' she murmured.

'Am I?'

'Dancing like this. You never said.'

'You never asked,' he replied. He had missed this, he realised. Not just Gwen, but this, an event, a Do, a dance partner. He wished he'd worn another shirt, something smarter, more festive.

The tune finished. He smiled at her, released her from his hold and turned to go back to his seat, but Doris touched his arm. 'Let's see what the next one is,' she said.

It was a waltz. 'Oh, I love a waltz,' she said.

He unzipped his cardigan and threw it onto a chair. Then they held each other again, and glided across the room. He liked dancing with her. She was a good dancer.

'Well, look at that,' Doris said.

He turned his head. The floor was empty, everyone was watching them dance. He closed his eyes for a moment, then he and Doris moved lightly, lightly round the room.

At the end, everyone clapped, and they bowed together, laughing.

'That calls for another cup of tea,' Doris said. She took

his hand as they walked over to the tea urn. 'I think this will be another good Christmas.'

He smiled in agreement.

The Christmas Choir

She went along for the company. She wasn't even sure she could sing. But the choirmaster declared she had a beautiful soprano voice. He even wanted her to do a duet with Bernard, a bass, for their special, festive evening.

It was the highlight of the season, with mulled wine and mince pies, and a twinkling tree. She and Bernard sang 'I'm dreaming of a White Christmas.'

After the concert, Bernard offered her a lift home. 'Even though it's over,' he said, as she climbed out of the car, 'would you like to sing some more?'

'Oh yes,' she smiled.

Father Christmas Fireman

Ronnie had always wanted to be a fireman. As a boy in the war he had watched from his bedroom window as fires raged through bombed buildings by the Hoffmann's factory. He had seen how distressed his mother became when the homes of friends and well-loved shops burned to the ground and he yearned to stop her tears. He ran out to help the fire wardens, doing odd jobs, collecting pails of water from neighbours, pointing out embers that were about to spark up, guiding other children away from danger. Sometimes the firemen shouted at him to get out of the way and then he would step back and watch how they handled the ladders, unreeled the hoses, called to each other where to go, where to stand, how to stay safe.

When he came back from National Service he cast around for what to do with his life. One morning, he stretched a newspaper across the fireplace in his mother's living room, trying to get the fire to draw. It wasn't working. Smoke filled the room. His mum said, 'You're doing it wrong. It's going to go out. But I'm not surprised - you always wanted to put fires out, not to start them.' And suddenly it all made sense. He would become a fireman.

He loved the job, all of it. The noise, the shouting, the camaraderie, the trust. From stepping across cracking beams in a smoking house, to releasing a toddler whose head was stuck in railings, he loved it all.

He and his comrades in the brigade sat in the canteen talking about the causes of fire, carelessly discarded cigarettes; the polyurethane foam that made furniture affordable but deadly; the paraffin heaters used in so many rooms that tipped and spilled and caused devastating damage and injuries.

And when the bell rang, they all sprang immediately into action. Shrugging on their jackets as they slid down the pole to the enormous vehicles waiting below. No risk was too great. Ron was always there, following commands, ensuring a smooth operation. His attitude and solid reliability were noticed and he rose through the ranks. But he always wanted to get in on the action and so when he gained promotion to station officer he chafed at the role he now had to play, guiding the process from the ground, but he knew it was the only way to ensure the safety of his men, and to effect a successful battle against the fire.

It was Christmas Eve. Ron's shift in the station in Waterhouse Lane was nearing the end and he was sorting out last minute instructions to hand over to the next team. He was looking forward to going home, and settling the kids down with their stockings at the foot of the bed and a plate of biscuits for Father Christmas in the living room. Then the call came - a fire in a large Victorian house on the Broomfield Road, a house of bed-sitting-rooms, a mile from the fire station. He threw off his overcoat.

Mick, his second in command, said, 'Ron, we've got this. Get out of here. You've been on since five o'clock this morning. It's Christmas Eve. Get off home.'

Ron said, 'It *is* Christmas Eve. That's why the sooner we do this the better for all of us.'

The fire was raging, up through the building, the windows glowing with flames or blotted with billowing smoke. As the fire engine pulled up an ambulance appeared, its blue lights flashing. A small crowd of bedraggled people, a young couple wearing slippers, a mother with her children in pyjamas, two men one still holding the evening newspaper, stood just outside the house, staring in fear and amazement at their homes burning on Christmas Eve. The ambulance driver leaped out and handed out blankets. Neighbours peeped out of windows, some even ventured into the street with chairs.

Ron assembled his team and like a well-rehearsed play, they slipped smoothly into their roles, unloading ladders and unrolling hosepipes. Ron went over to the mother and her children. 'Are there any more people inside?' he asked urgently.

'I-I don't think so.' She looked round helplessly, pulling the children closer.

The man with the newspaper said, 'We called out to everyone, we were shouting the house down. I think they all came out.' Ron, as the station officer, directed the operation. Mick and two men leaned a ladder against the wall. Ron told them to go into the ground floor and check the safety of the building. They disappeared into the house. Other men began spraying the whole building with water. Ron watched. Watching was the part of the job he hated most.

He moved across to the young couple. Their arms were wrapped around each other. 'Are you sure the building is empty?'

'I don't know,' the young man said. 'I think – someone said once that there was an old man on the top floor. I don't know. I've never seen him.' The girl burst into tears.

There was the clanging of an approaching fire engine. An extra team had arrived from a station outside the town.

Quickly and efficiently, Ron brought the newly arrived station officer up to speed.

The house was beginning to complain. There was a crack from behind the front door and the shouts of firemen to each other. 'Careful on the staircase!' 'Watch those beams!'

He turned to the new man. 'Right, you can take over command now. I'm going in.' The new man frowned. 'I'm going up to join my men,' Ron said. 'With a blaze like this you can never have a big enough team. There's no time to lose.'

He leaped onto the ladder and began climbing up the side of the building. The walls were steaming from the heat and the water being played up them. Climbing higher he reached the window of the second floor, then the third floor and the fourth. He stared in to each room. Through the smoke he could see the shadows of his men, moving through the house, steadily and carefully, checking for gas leaks, checking the structure, searching the house. As he reached the fifth-floor window the heat was intense. He pulled his axe from his belt and smashed the window and climbed into a room full of smoke. From below he could hear the shouts of his team. In the billowing smoke and with the roar of the flames and rush of the water hoses, he only had a vague idea of where they were. But he knew he was alone on this floor.

With the roar of the fire in his ears he climbed into the room, shouting to check if anyone was there. He shone his torch into the corners. There was no-one. He made his way onto the landing, where an old mattress was smouldering, letting out clouds of rancid smoke. There were four more doors on the landing. Three were open. He shouted and turned his torch into each one. They were all empty. He heard the creaking roar of wood yearning to move and Mick's voice calling all the men out of the building. The cracking sound of fire rose louder and smoke billowed ever thicker. He looked up and he could tell the roof was about to give. Breathing now with difficulty he turned to the closed door. He hammered on the thin wood. There was no reply. He tried the handle. The door was locked. He raised his foot and kicked open the door. 'Hello?' he shouted. 'Hello?" Flames were licking round his thick boots. He moved into the room, squinting in the darkness, training his torch into the corners, making out the form of a table, a bed, a sink. And then an arm. A wheelchair. In the eery glow of the torch he could see an elderly man sitting alone, helpless, trembling. On his head was a paper crown from a Christmas cracker.

'Hello mate,' said Ron. 'Good to see you.'

'I could say the same,' the man whispered.

'Who else is here?' Ron asked quickly.

'It's just me,' the old man sighed, almost breathless.

'Are you sure?' Ron said, his eyes scouring the room. 'Who did you pull your cracker with?'

'I get this hat out every year, for Christmas. To get in the party spirit.'

'Oh, right,' Ron said. 'Well, that's good, but I think the party's over for today.'

'What do you mean?'

'It's time to go, mate.'

'But my things. My hat.' He raised a trembling hand to his head.

'Don't worry. There's plenty more crackers downstairs. In fact, a lot of them are coming up the stairs right now to find you.' There was the sound of splintering wood. A whoosh of air caused the door to bang against the wall. Smoke and flame billowed in.

The old man laughed, a thin, wheezing sound. 'Fireworks. I always put on a good party.'

'Well, this party over,' Ron said. Sweat dripped down his face. He leant forward, thrust his hands under the old man's arms and, grunting 'This one's just begun,' lifted the man high and threw him over his shoulder. 'Hold on!' he shouted. He could feel the faint pressure of the man on his back. 'What's your name by the way?'

'Arthur.'

'OK, Arthur. Grab onto my belt! Watch your fingers with the axe. And I don't know if you're any good at holding your breath, but now might be a good time to start practising.' Then Ron and the man Arthur made their slow way across the smoke-filled room, out onto the landing, past the burning mattress, and the flames licking up the stairs, over the now sodden floor of the room to the window where the ladder awaited. With an effort, taking care of Arthur's frail body, Ron lifted his leg over the window sill and found the top rung of the ladder. Then holding onto the window frame, he swung his other leg out and onto the ladder, and slowly and carefully Ron and Arthur made their way down to the ground.

There was a smattering of applause from the watching crowd, and then an enormous roar from the house as the roof caved in, sending a shower of sparks into the night sky.

As Arthur was tucked into a blanket and lifted into the waiting ambulance, he gave a thin smile. 'You saved my life,' he whispered to Ron. 'You saved my life.'

Ron tapped his helmet in response and turned to take charge of the next stage of the operation.

Later, telling the story, Ron would lean forward, holding the bowl of his pipe. 'Best Christmas present ever, to save a man's life. And what's more, I got home before Father Christmas had come. He left a lot of soot on the plate of biscuits, that Christmas night.'

The Christmas Note

In the canteen, drinking egg-nog, Janet leaned across to the next table and said, 'Could you stop smoking? It's a filthy habit. We're breathing it in!'

As Steve left, a piece of paper fluttered down onto Janet's saucer. There was a telephone number. And a drawing of mistletoe.

She didn't ring. But a week later, at the Christmas party, he was there again, smiling and chatting. Not smoking. He came up to her and said, 'I stopped smoking but you didn't ring.'

'Really?' she asked, laughing. 'You did that for me?' She leaned up and kissed him.

Later they married.

The Christmas Cookery Lesson

1963

They had cookery on Tuesday afternoons. On Monday evening Carol had to go to the shops to buy the ingredients she would need. Usually it was butter, eggs, or vanilla essence. Her mum said it was scandalous they had to use good food on a lesson. 'The school should provide it,' she said. 'They put it on the timetable, they should pay for the things you need.' She looked at Carol's face. 'I know. I'm not making a fuss. We always love what you cook. It's just it's a bit expensive every week. We'll never use those cloves you bought for the apple pie. Unless you develop a toothache.'

When they did something with meat she had to go to the Parade on the Main Road, where Major's, the butcher's, sat in the middle of the row of shops.

She liked the boy who worked in Major's. He was a bit of a rocker, with his pointed shoes, and his slicked back greasy hair, but he always gave her a smile, and after he'd weighed the meat and worked out the price, he always chucked in a little bit more. Which was very nice but it upset her measurements for the class. She didn't know how to tell him, because she liked that he did it. She didn't know his name till she heard Mr Major the owner call to him once, when he was weighing out her sausage meat for Scotch eggs. His name was Alec.

'So what's the class cooking up this week?' he would ask, after he had realised she only came in for her cookery lesson ingredients.

One week it was shepherd's pie. 'Very nice,' he said.

'Lamb's mince,' she said.

'I know what shepherd's pie is, missus.'

She laughed. 'Sorry, I didn't mean that. It's just our teacher was making such a big thing of it last week. "We are not making Cottage Pie, we are making Shepherd's Pie. So please tell your mothers we shall require the flesh of the sheep."'

He laughed. 'Did she really say that?'

'I know, unbelievable!'

There was a pause and they looked at each other.

As he balanced a handful of mince on the scales, he said, 'Do you ever go into the Compasses? Down the road?'

'Sometimes.' She didn't know why she'd said that, she never went to the Compasses.

'I'll buy you a drink if I see you in there.'

'Oh yeah?' She raised her eyebrows and hoped she wasn't blushing.

'I'm usually in there on a Friday night. About 7.'

'Well, I might see you there,' she said. She walked to the door with the bag of mince. There was a cough behind her. It was Mr Major.

'Excuse me, love. I think you've forgotten something.'

She hadn't paid. Now she really was blushing. Blindly she rushed to the small kiosk where Mrs Major sat throughout the day, taking the money. She was half aware that Alec was studiously tidying the display of mince, not looking at her.

'Of course we can't go,' she said to her best friend Angie, when she told her. 'He thinks I'm a thief, walking out of the shop. He probably thinks I was chatting with him to cause a diversion, so I could leave without paying.'

'Of course we can go,' Angie said. 'He knows it was a mistake. If the worst comes to the worst he'll think you did it on purpose, to make him notice you because you fancy him.'

'He can't think that! That's terrible.' Carol cringed with embarrassment. How could she fancy him? He was a rocker. She was a mod.

They didn't go.

Now, three weeks later, it was nearly Christmas, it was her last term at school and her last cookery lesson. The cookery teacher had chosen a recipe for pigs in blankets.

She walked into the shop, frozen from the biting wind outside. Inside the shop was warm with the fresh woody smell of sawdust from the shavings on the floor. A red and gold sign on the window of Mrs Major's kiosk said, 'Happy Christmas to all our customers,' and the plaster pig's head on the back wall had a wreath of holly with red berries around its neck.

Alec's face lit up as she walked in, and her heart leaped, relieved. Perhaps he'd forgotten the last time she'd seen him, but then he stopped smiling and frowned as if he'd suddenly remembered. She'd been rude and oh goodness, he thought she was a thief. Well, she wasn't a thief. She just hadn't realised she hadn't paid. She had nothing to be ashamed of, it was his problem. So when he approached her, his face still blank, she said, 'Shall I wait till he's ready to serve me?' She nodded her head towards Mr Major who was cutting through a large piece of meat with noisy whacks of the knife.

'Why, do you want him to serve you?' He looked surprised.

'No! I thought you might not want to serve me,' she

said, uncertainly. She could feel her cheeks reddening.

'Why not?'

'You know!' she whispered.

His eyes widened. She almost stamped her foot. He must know what she meant.

'Is there a problem, Alec?' Mr Major called across the room. Mrs Major in the kiosk was watching them both.

'No!' Alec said quickly.

'No!' Carol shook her head violently.

'What would you like?' Alec said politely, loudly. 'Are you OK?' he murmured.

'Yes! Why wouldn't I be?' she shot back.

'I don't know.' He shook his head, bewildered. 'I just thought you looked a bit ... I don't know ... fierce.'

'Me?' This was awful. She didn't know how to make it right.

'Alec?' Mr Major said, wrapping chops in greaseproof paper.

'I'm on it!' he replied and turned to her.

'We're making pigs in blankets,' she said, desperately.

Something happened. He smiled. 'Oh really?'

'Yes, really.' Why was he smiling?

'Good job you didn't come in yesterday.'

She looked at him.

'I'd never heard of them. But you're the third person today who's come in wanting sausages and bacon. I had to ask Mrs Major. She'd seen it in a magazine.' They grinned at each other.

'I thought you were ... fed up with me,' she said softly.

'What made you think that?'

'You stopped smiling when I came in just now.'

'Well – I didn't want to look too eager.' He touched her arm, lightly.

The touch hummed through her body. She was so pleased it was all right.

'So how much do you want?' He glanced over at Mr Major and nodded, then looked at her, smiling and she smiled back, knowing he meant that he had to look professional in front of his boss. She giggled.

She took out the sheet of paper with the recipe and handed it to him.

He studied it, then went through a door at the back of the shop. She imagined large freezers full of meat and Alec pulling out huge joints, selecting the right sausages, a nice side of bacon, in his white coat, his hair flopping into his eyes.

He came back smiling and she watched him weigh the sausages and the bacon and add a rasher. He looked at her over the scales and winked. He wrapped it all up and she took the parcel over to the kiosk and gave Mrs Major the money. Mrs Major smiled and said, 'Another one making pigs in blankets! Let me know how they turn out. I might give them a try myself.'

Carol nodded and turned to go. She glanced round the shop but Alec wasn't there. She felt disappointed. Oh, she knew he was a rocker, with his greased back hair and his pointed cowboy boots. And she was a mod in her neat skirts and moccasin shoes. But there was a gnawing in her stomach, a feeling of things unfinished. She'd wanted to tell him she was leaving school, that she would never be back for ingredients for her cookery lessons. She'd wanted to see what he'd say.

As she reached the door, she heard Alec's voice. 'Hey!' She stopped. He came up to her and pulled open the door. A blast of cold wind blew into the shop. On the street a group of carol singers were singing God Rest Ye Merry Gentlemen. 'I don't know your name,' he said. 'You can't give a girl a Christmas kiss if you don't know her name.'

She looked at him in surprise. She knew Angie would have made some smart remark, like 'Good job you don't know her name then,' or 'You couldn't give this girl a kiss even if you did know her name.' But she said simply, 'It's Carol.'

'Happy Christmas Carol,' he murmured and kissed her on the cheek.

Suddenly she wanted to say, 'Do you still go to the Compasses? Shall I see you there?' but Mr Major was laughing. 'Watch out, Alec,' he called. 'You can't give all the girls a kiss.'

'He's messing about,' Alec said. 'You're the first girl I've kissed. The only girl.' Was he blushing?

This was all too embarrassing. She stepped out into the street. 'Oh, don't forget this,' he said and handed back the shopping list. She shoved it into the bottom of the bag.

When she was at home, unpacking the shopping, the list was stuck to the package of meat. She pulled at it and it fluttered to the floor. She picked it up. He'd written a message 'Remember to wrap up warm, you and your pigs. Come by for more blankets any time.' Her heart quickened. He'd written that, to her. She smoothed out the paper. She smiled. A rocker had written a note to a mod. That was unbelievable.

It didn't mean anything of course. Carefully she folded the list in half – she needed the list of ingredients for the class tomorrow. She tore off the piece with the message. She studied it carefully. What did it mean? Her and her pigs? Was he being rude? Should she show it to Angie? She was going over to Angie's later, to talk about dress patterns. No, best not. Angie would laugh. Say she was mad. They could never meet anywhere except the butcher's shop, her in her suede coat, him in his leather jacket with chains and studs. She hadn't seen his jacket – she'd never seen him in anything but his white coat, stained with blood - but she'd imagined it. As she'd imagined sitting on the back of his motorbike. Going really fast – doing a ton, tearing down the by-pass at a hundred miles an hour. No, it could never happen. She screwed up the little message and threw it away.

On Friday evening, when they were on the bus into town she said casually to Angie. 'We could get off at the Compasses, for a laugh.'

Angie said, 'We could, but then we'd have to walk the rest of the way.'

'But we could,' Carol persisted.

'Oh,' Angie said, 'the penny's just dropped. All right, let's go and see Mr Meat.'

The pub wasn't busy. There were two bars and he wasn't in the public. 'Let's try the saloon,' Angie said.

The saloon was Christmassy with green and red decorations draped across the ceiling and bunches of mistletoe hanging over the doors. A fire was burning in the grate, giving out waves of heat. In a corner Carol was shocked to see Mr Major, puffing on a thick cigar, while Mrs Major sipped something yellow, that looked like advocaat. They both waved at Carol.

'Well, there's one Mr Meat,' Angie said.

'That's not really the one I was hoping to bump into,' Carol murmured.

'Do you want to stay? To see if he comes? He might be in the toilet.'

Carol shuddered. 'We'd have to talk Mr and Mrs Major.' She looked hopelessly round the bar. 'It's not worth it. He couldn't say anything in front of his boss.'

'Well, he's not going to say he loves you tonight!' Angie said.

'I know. But he's not here. He's not coming.'

They walked out into the frosty night, and trudged into town. Carol was silent with disappointment. 'Cheer up,' Angie said, linking her arm through Carol's. 'At least getting off the bus at the Compasses meant the fare was cheaper.'

Carol nodded. 'At least that.'

The sound of a motor bike engine faded behind them.

The Christmas Play

It was the school nativity play. Graham's dad had made a 2D donkey of balsawood, with one big brown eye. Graham was 10. He was Joseph, taking the donkey to Bethlehem. The donkey came on stage first, pushed by Graham, then Mary, in her mum's blue dress. She tripped and fell into the stable.

A shepherd rushed over and took her arm, helping her up.

'Hey!' Graham shouted. 'That's my wife!'

'You only care about the donkey,' Mary said. 'I'm going with him.'

'But that's not the story. What will happen to the world?'

'Let's see,' said Mary and left.

The Christmas Affair

As he said hello, he heard the sound of someone pressing Button A and the four pennies falling into the coin receptacle in the phone box. His heart sank.

'Tony? Tony? Can't you change the arrangement?'

'I...'

'If I don't see you tonight, I shan't see you for two weeks,' Sheila sobbed.

He sighed. He knew he should say, 'Let's not stop at two weeks, let's make it forever!' and slam down the phone and be done with it. But he couldn't do that. When Sheila was in one of these moods, she might do anything. She could weep and wail till someone asked her what was wrong. And she was quite capable of telling them. 'Well, you'll see me at your mother's,' he said, trying to inject a friendly lilt into his voice.

'That's hardly the same,' she snapped. 'You'll be with my sister. Mum will be all over her and the grandchildren. And you. The perfect happy family. I'll be in the kitchen, buttering bread.'

'Oh, well...'

And I shan't even be able to kiss you under the mistletoe.'

'Surely that wouldn't hurt!'

'It would hurt me. I wouldn't be able to stop myself. I'd want to run my hands through your hair and then all down your back and then I'd want to pull you close to me and you'd be so pleased to be with me. Anyone would be able to see that. Mmm.' She moaned softly. 'Can you imagine?'

Oh, he should have put the phone down quicker. She always did this, got him all hot and bothered, got him right where she wanted him. 'Yes, yes I can imagine.' He knew it was stupid but he couldn't stop himself thinking of her soft skin, her full lips, that strange perfume she wore, exotic and ordinary at the same time.

'Can't you?' she whispered. 'Can't you come, just for a few minutes?' It was that husky tone of voice that she only used when they were alone together.

In his head he ran through all the preparations that would be required, working out his excuses, the timing, explaining the scent on the clothes he was wearing. Could he use the office party again? Had he already told Margaret the firm was cutting back and not having a party this year?

'And I've got your Christmas present!' Sheila said petulantly.

He knew how she must look as she spoke in that tone, her soft red lips, a slight sheen on them as she pressed them together, her eyes flashing. He wanted to kiss her there and then.

'And don't you have something for me?' she breathed, her mouth close to the phone.

'Oh, of course.' Now he had to add shopping to the list of things to organise. Because he knew it was useless to deny her – or himself. He would have to see her tonight. He wanted to see her.

'I'm wearing my pink jumper,' she murmured. 'The one you like so much, the very tight one.' She pronounced the word 'tight' slowly, emphasising the 't's.

His body strained to be with her.

'What are you wearing?' she breathed.

He cleared his throat. 'The usual, I'm afraid. The blue shirt and – and the brown trousers.'

She laughed. 'Those baggy old things? Well, it doesn't matter. We'll have them off in no time.'

'Oh Sheila,' he moaned, half complaining. 'Stop.'

'So, six o'clock in our usual spot?'

'Yes, yes, look, I must go now.'

'All right, darling. You won't be sorry.' She blew kisses down the phone.

They had found a little shed affair at the back of the park on the west side of the town, where no-one ever came, and Sheila always brought two blankets and a pillow, and tonight a couple of candles.

Her gift to him was a tie-pin, which he could never wear because he didn't wear tie-pins and he certainly wouldn't wear a tie-pin with a stallion's head on it, however flattering it might be. His gift to her was a token to redeem at Clarke's, the book shop in town. They had been on the point of closing as he dashed in. Sheila would of course receive another gift tomorrow, from him and Margaret and the boys, which was, he knew, a box of biscuits. A book token was a little more personal than that.

Now as they rearranged their clothing and she wiped lipstick from his cheek, she mused on what book she might choose. 'How about the Kama Sutra?' she giggled, her initial reaction of disappointment now giving way to her fantasies. It's what he liked about her. Her bad moods never lasted long. She didn't enjoy them any more than he did. 'Or something even dirtier – what's that one? – Lady Chatterley and her Lover.' She rolled the word lover round her tongue.

'I don't know if they'd sell it to you.' He smoothed his tie down and tucked the ends into the space between the third and fourth button on his shirt. He had seen a lad in technical drawing wear his tie like that and he thought it looked quite dashing.

'Well, put it on,' Sheila said. 'Your new tie-pin!'

'All right. Just for five minutes. I'll have to take it

off before I get there.' It was going to be hard enough to explain his late arrival without the snorting nostrils of a manly beast on his chest.

'Oh, Tony baby,' she crooned, 'you are such a worrywart.' She ran her finger over his lips. Then she leaped up, suddenly all efficiency. She folded the blankets and put them in her basket. 'Give me five? Ten minutes?' she said, 'And then you set off.'

She kissed him on the nose. 'I'll see you at mum's. But I'll be remembering just now!' She nuzzled her cheek against his and she was gone.

He was surprised when Sheila answered the door, as soon as he rang the bell. 'Come in,' she said excitedly, leaning in for a kiss. 'Don't worry, Margaret 's not even here.'

'Thank god for that,' he muttered. Then in a clear voice he said, 'What do you mean she's not here, where is she? Are the boys here?'

'Nope.' Sheila took his mac and hung it up.

'Oh, I thought it might be Margaret.' Dorothy, his mother-in-law, appeared in the hallway just as he remembered the tie-pin. It was still on his tie, glittering in the reflection of the Christmas lights in the hallway. It was an effort to keep his hand casually in his pocket.

'Mm, nice tie-pin,' Sheila murmured, lightly touching

his shirt, on the spot she had bitten him an hour before. His stomach contracted with desire.

'Did she ring you at the office?' Dorothy said. She held a jar of pickled red cabbage which she handed to him.

Automatically he opened it for her, then passed it back. He didn't know any other family that ate salad for the evening meal the night before Christmas. He never enjoyed it. 'No, I haven't heard from her all day. But then, I never do.'

Sheila was pushing him gently towards the doorway to the lounge, where the mistletoe hung. 'How about a Christmas kiss?' she said.

'Sheila!' Dorothy said sharply. 'At least let's sort out the Margaret business first.'

'Oh, she won't care,' said Sheila, an unnatural brightness in her eyes.

'Whether she will or not, is not the point. She's never late. It's just not like her.' Dorothy was opening and closing the jar of red cabbage.

Sheila sighed. 'Oh, I forgot.' She delved into her handbag. 'I wonder if this might explain it.'

'What is it?' Dorothy snatched the pink envelope. The word 'Mum' was written on the front. Tony recognised Margaret's writing.

'It was on the mat when I came in,' Sheila said. They both stared at her. 'Well, don't look at me, I don't know what it says.' Tony wasn't sure he believed her. He could see that the envelope had been opened already, there was a small tear in the flap and it was stuck down unevenly.

Dorothy stared at the envelope then opened it and took out a folded piece of matching pink paper. Her eyes moved quickly down the page. 'Oh my god.' Her hand was trembling at her mouth. 'Oh my god.'

'What? What is it?' Tony said.

Dorothy thrust the paper at him, then turned and rushed back to the kitchen.

'What on earth?' He frowned at Sheila as he smoothed out the paper. She widened her eyes, innocently.

Dear Mum, he read

I know this will come as a shock, and I probably should have told Tony first but I know he'll be with you when you open this (if he's not late, as usual), and it's always hard to find the right words.

The thing is the boys and I aren't going to be spending Christmas with you. We shall be in Benidorm, where we went on holiday in July. I think I told you what a nice time we had. What I didn't tell you was about Carlos, the waiter in the hotel who was so good with the boys, and taught Robby to swim, and showed them the best places on the beach for rock pools. He was especially helpful as Tony kept disappearing to make 'business calls' as he called them. Well, one thing led to another and we kept in touch after the holiday and suffice to say you've got a little Spanish bambino (that's Spanish) on the way and I'm hoping for a girl.

Tell Tony we're all well, and I'll be in touch after Christmas. I'll think of you on Christmas day eating your chicken. Carlos says we'll be having paella (that's Spanish).

Love Margaret and the boys.

Tony sank onto the sofa. Sheila threw herself down next to him. 'What does it say?' she said innocently. 'Show me!'

Weakly he held out the piece of paper. Sheila looked at it briefly, then snorted. 'Well, there you are! And you were so worried! We might as well have that kiss under the mistletoe now.'

'Benidorm,' he murmured. 'All that time I spent ringing you.'

'I missed you so much,' she crooned softly.

'And he was such a friendly guy,' Tony said. He put his head in his hands.

'Well, at least we can eat now, surely,' Sheila said. 'Good job we're having salad or everything would have been spoiled. That's Margaret all over.'

He had often mocked Margaret for this strange, cold, family tradition. Now it seemed to him the most poignant of all possible meals, the jar of red cabbage he had just opened, the mustardy piccalilli, the bottle of salad cream, the slices of ham, the hard-boiled eggs, the thinly cut bread and butter, even the soggy lettuce. How could he eat it without Margaret? He stood up abruptly, causing Sheila to topple sideways.

'Oh, I say!' she exclaimed.

'I can't stay,' he cried, pulling off the tie-pin. 'I've got to find her before she makes a huge mistake. A baby? She's having a baby? And she thinks it's his?'

'Well, you two don't *do* it any more, do you?' Sheila said, wildly.

'Sheila!' Dorothy was standing in the doorway. 'What are you talking about?'

Sheila gave unnatural laugh. 'That's what he told ... us ... last Christmas. Don't you remember, mum? We were playing charades. *Three Men and a Baby.*'

'It's what you wanted to hear,' he hissed at Sheila. She followed him into the hall. He was trying to find his mac, pulling coats and hats aside, throwing scarves onto the floor. 'I've got to go. I'm sorry, Dorothy, I'm sure tea would have been lovely. I'm going to Benidorm. I've got to get her back. And my baby. Don't you understand? I love my wife! It's Christmas!'

As the door closed behind him, Sheila was shaking. Dorothy looked at her for a long moment. 'Well, we shan't be playing charades, but there'll be more ham for you!' she said. 'Or if you like –' Her tone became softer '- let's have a change of menu. Margaret's not here with her demand for salad.' She turned and walked back to the kitchen 'There's those sausages in the fridge. We shan't need pigs in blankets tomorrow. Tony won't be here and he's the only one who likes them. I could put the sausages under the grill and do some chips. We can even open that new bottle of ketchup. Let's have a different Christmas Eve for once.'

Sheila dabbed at her eyes. 'That sounds delicious.' She stood quietly in the doorway of the kitchen, then she laughed. 'You've got to hand it to Margaret. She knows how to pick her men.' She walked towards the fridge. 'I'll get out the sausages.'

The Christmas Cake

Every year mum made a Christmas cake. Every year the fruit sank to the bottom. Everyone laughed and said how hopeless she was at baking.

Mum had never baked a thing before she got married. Her mum had died when she was just 16.

My dad left her after 24 years, went to live with her best friend and her children. The next Christmas Eve I went to visit. He and I were in the kitchen, doing the washing up.

'Your mother was impossible to live with,' he said, handing me a dripping plate, 'but I miss her Christmas cake.'

The Christmas Kiss

On Christmas Eve anything was possible. Everyone was out on Christmas Eve, dressed in their best. Everyone was looking for a Christmas kiss. And this Christmas Eve fell on a Saturday so there was a dance at the Corn Exchange and Georgie Fame was playing.

The Corn Exchange was dark and cavernous, with dusty floorboards and dark, non-conformist chairs lining the walls. There was the smell of perfume and after-shave and the crunchy smell of new suede coats. And as always, the exotic mix of strangers from out of town and boys we knew. But tonight there was a layer of Christmas excitement, people in shiny make-up, bright red lipstick and glittering eye-shadow. Some girls had tinsel draped round their necks, a few boys had sprigs of mistletoe in their top pocket. The evening was wrapped in shining possibilities tied up with the bow of good cheer.

We made our way across the hall to the ladies' toilets, and handed our suede coats to Brenda, the Saturday night coat-manager. I noticed Sandra had a sparkly brooch pinned to her cardigan and I wished I'd thought of that.

'Hello girls,' Brenda said. Brenda was an older motherly woman, who nonetheless worked in the Orpheus when she wasn't at the Corn Exchange. The Orpheus was the mods' coffee bar where we spent most of our evenings, when the Corn Exchange wasn't open.

Brenda pinned raffle tickets to the lining of our suedes and gave the other halves to Sandra. The prize would be to get our coats back at the end of the evening.

In the washroom I looked at my reflection in the mirror. I was growing my hair. Tonight I had it parted on the side with a pony-tail pinned at the back. I wasn't wearing anything new or even vaguely fashionable, with my fine-knit jumper and straight skirt, but I knew I looked good. Black and grey was a mod look, safe but classic. And on Christmas Eve it didn't matter that I didn't have anyone special who might appreciate it, because tonight anyone might appreciate it.

We moved away from the wash basins as more girls came in to the room, bringing waves of fresh new perfume, in clothes that made me yearn for higher wages in my Saturday job.

As we walked back into the hall, Georgie Fame's group, the Blue Flames, were setting up their equipment. People were already clustering in front of the stage, jostling for the best spot.

'So what are we going to do tonight?'

'Have a good Christmas Eve.'

We laughed and wove our way through the room. The place was filling up with noisy, excited people, waiting for good music, good dancing, a starry Christmas night out. We nodded to those we knew, waved to those on the other side of the hall and watched boys in lean sharp suits stepping forward to dance, as the first blasting trumpet notes of *Harlem Shuffle* filled the hall.

'I like this one,' I said. 'I might buy this one.' My dad had recently bought a record player for the family.

'Your third record,' Sandra said, sarcastically. They had had a record player for years and had piles of singles and LPs, Elvis Presley and Roy Orbison, Connie Francis and even Ruby Murray. 'Do you want to stay and listen?' she asked.

'No, I'll wait till I've bought it.'

'Then let's go up the Fleece. I'll buy you a gin and bitter lemon and then you can come back and talk to anyone you feel like.'

We walked out of the hall, down the steps and into the street. There was a shout. It came from a white car with a black roof. It was Sandra's boyfriend Danny in a shiny Austin A40. He opened the driver's door and leaned across the roof of the car and shouted again. 'Sandra!'

'Well, look what the cat dragged in!' Sandra said. Danny had been in prison for 6 months and she hadn't expected to see him before the New Year.

'Perhaps he wanted to give you a Christmas surprise,' I said.

'I'll give him a Christmas surprise.'

We walked over to the car. There was the delicate, sweet smell of his aftershave, Old Spice. A lot of boys in Chelmsford wore Old Spice. It made me think of soft, puffy cheeks, and sweet beery breath. 'What are you up to?' Danny said as if we'd seen him that afternoon in the Orpheus and he'd put 'He's a Rebel' on the juke box and Brenda had tried to get us to buy another cup of coffee, like any Saturday. He looked quite fashionable for once, wearing a tan sheepskin coat. Sheepskin coats were coming in. Sandra was staring at him. I could see she was wondering why he hadn't told her he was coming home and trying to decide how to handle the situation.

I looked into the car. Charlie Daniels was in the passenger seat holding a box of crackers, and his brother Harry sat in the back wearing a paper crown. Charlie and Harry worked on the buildings, but they also had a 'night job' stealing lead from the roofs of local buildings. When they came into the Orpheus in their big work boots, someone would put 'Up on the Roof' on the juke box. Charlie would play along, waving his hands in the air, in time to the music. Like the rest of him, his hands looked hard and tough. I wondered what it would feel like if he stroked your face with those work-worn hands.

Once Charlie had come into the Milk Bar where I worked on Saturdays. He bought a cup of tea for sixpence. He paid with half a crown, and told me to keep the change. A two-bob tip was the best I'd ever had. Sandra said keeping those two shillings meant I'd received the profits of a crime, but I knew he earned some, legitimate, money on the buildings, so it could have come from there.

'Except that last night the lead on the roof of the Methodist church was nicked,' she'd said darkly.

'To get half a crown for it the next day would be quick,' I said.

'That's what you think. Buy us a coffee and I'll keep my mouth shut when the police interview me,' she said. This was the kind of conversation Sandra and I had.

But ever since that day I'd always felt that Charlie and I had a special relationship, although he'd never spoken to me, before or since. I quite liked Charlie.

Now he turned to Harry. 'Are we stopping? I want to see the group.' He tossed the box of crackers into the back of the car and climbed out. He was wearing a long maroon suede coat.

'Mmm, nice,' Sandra murmured.

'Hello girls,' he said. 'Coming inside?'

Sandra and I exchanged a look.

Danny said, 'Go on Charlie and take little Linda with you. She looks like she could do with a bit of excitement.' He meant it rudely, but I didn't care. The thought of walking into the Corn Exchange with Charlie was almost a Christmas wish come true.

'What about me?' Sandra said.

'I need to talk to you,' Danny said. Sandra rolled her eyes. Danny was so unpredictable.

'What do you want to talk about?' she asked. He might want to talk about something ordinary like whether he should become a postman or it could be something like goodbye for ever, which would ruin anyone's Christmas.

'I can't say it here,' he said. 'Get in. Let's go to the Compasses. They're having a party up there.'

Sandra stood on the edge of the kerb. Harry pushed down the back window of the car and said, 'Here. Have a cracker.' He handed a long thin tube of red crepe paper to her. I expected we'd pull it together, find a joke, fight over the hat. But she held it like a police officer with a truncheon, tapping it into the palm of her hand. 'I'm out with Linda,' she said. 'I haven't heard from you for two weeks, and you certainly never said you were coming home.'

'But Linda's with Charlie now.'

'Am I?' My breath quickened. Was I really?

Sandra looked at me. 'I don't know.' She was hesitating.

'See you at the bus station?' I said. It was where our evenings always ended, before we caught the bus home together.

'Maybe,' she murmured. She turned back to Danny. 'How much money have you got?'

'What kind of question's that?'

'Have you got enough money to buy the drinks?'

'Believe it or not, I've got ten quid.' He waved a note in the air.

'You've got a lot of explaining to do.'

'Get in the car and I'll explain everything.' He grinned at her and I knew she would go.

Under her breath she muttered, 'If I'm not at the bus station, go home because I'll be at the police station charged with grievous bodily harm.'

'OK,' I said. She rummaged in her bag and gave me the raffle ticket for my coat, then with a final grimace, she stepped into the car. I watched as they lurched away. Danny had never taken a driving test.

Charlie took my hand. It felt just as I had imagined, his fingers were hard and calloused as if they would find it difficult to bend, but the palm was warm and the pad of his thumb was quite soft. 'What's your name again?' he said.

'Linda.' Sometimes I wished my name was Solange or Françoise, something exotic and full of promise. A name that people would remember.

'Linda! Lin-da,' he said, making it sound rich and exciting. 'Come on, girl, let's get on that dance floor.'

I held out my wrist to the men on the door to show them my entry stamp. They scarcely looked at it and waved us in.

In the hall the stage was still being set up for the big star. *Going to a Go-Go* was playing on the turntable. I loved its twanging guitars and the pounding drum beat. I wondered if I should buy this one too.

I knew Charlie would dance in his coat. I knew that even people from London or Ipswich who had come to see Georgie Fame would think he was stylish. What I didn't know was if we'd be able to dance together properly. There were so many different dances and dance steps.

'OK, let's go,' Charlie said. He was still holding my hand. He put his other arm about my waist and pushed me gently round. We were going to jive. This was dangerous ground. Sandra and I practised our jive for hours, making sure our neat controlled moves worked together and stayed precise and mod. But what kind of jive would Charlie do? He surely wouldn't do a rocker's rock and roll jive, with skirts swirling and hair flying. Would he?

Yes, he would. He was leaning backwards, moving on his heels with his toes pointing outwards, clicking his fingers, pushing me this way and that. I twirled and swayed following his moves Sometimes we twirled together and we both laughed when it was successful.

Occasionally, as you had to when you were jiving, he held me close, before pushing me away again. But once he didn't push me away, he kept me there, and looked at me, and gradually we stopped moving, standing in the middle of the hall, as the tambourines rattled and Smokey Robinson urged us to come on now and the mods around us continued dancing the Block and the Bang. I didn't know what he wanted. He pulled me even closer. I could feel him all down my body. The music was fading and the song ended.

'You're a good dancer,' I said. 'I don't normally jive with people I don't know.'

'We make a good pair,' he said. He looked round the hall. Was he bored? Was he looking for another partner? He turned back to me. As if he'd read my mind he said, 'I'm just looking for Harry. He's picking up a new car tonight. It's a Jag.' My eyes widened. He laughed. 'You're sweet. Do you want to come up West with us? We could be up there in an hour.'

I laughed. Was he mad? 'I think you're mistaking me for someone whose mum *wouldn't* kill her if she drove to London in the middle of the night. Not to mention Sandra.'

'Sure?' I could smell his breath, the spearmint of chewing gum. 'Really sure?'

I wondered what someone called Solange would say. 'Sure,' I said. 'But I'd like to.'

'You work in the Milk Bar, don't you?'

I nodded.

'I've seen you in there, in your little apron, carrying the sandwiches and the pies.'

I wondered if he remembered the tip. 'I've seen you too,' I said. 'You gave me a tip once.'

'Did I? I hope it was a good one.'

'It was,' I said, sadly. The tip obviously hadn't meant the same to him as it had to me. 'It was two bob.'

'Oh, that was you!' He hugged me tight. 'Of course it was. You smiled at me so nicely. I was having a really bad day.' He shook his head. 'You cheered me up. I thought what a sweet kind girl you were. Are you always so nice?'

'Always,' I said. 'I'm kind to animals too.'

'I hope you spent the money wisely.'

'I bought a pair of stockings.' He was still holding me close.

'You wouldn't be wearing them now, would you?' he murmured, his hand sliding down my back.

'It was a long time ago,' I said. 'They got laddered when I had to rescue a kitten from a tree.'

'Shame. I'd like to have seen them.... I mean that.'

'I bet you would.'

He laughed. 'Baby, you could rescue me from a tree anytime.'

'Make sure I'm not wearing my best stockings.'

'I would love to.' He laughed again, a deep rasping laugh. 'See? We get on like a house on fire. We can dance, you can smile. What more do we want?'

Shared interests, I thought. I wanted to ask him what newspaper he read, but it wasn't the right moment, and actually I didn't care. This was Christmas Eve. Nothing was real.

'All right, if you won't come with me tonight, how about next Friday? We could go to the flicks.'

'How old are you?' I asked cautiously.

'Nineteen,' he said slowly.

I didn't believe him. 'I'm fifteen,' I said.

His right eyebrow rose slightly. 'Seriously? When you sixteen?'

'In three months.'

He looked up as if he was doing a calculation. He sighed. 'All right. See you in three months.'

I frowned. I wanted to say 'Me being sixteen won't make any difference.'

'Just kidding!' he said. 'I can't let a nice little dancer like you get away. See you on Friday. 7 o'clock?' I began to smile. Charlie was a big mod in Chelmsford, he had the clothes, the shoes, the hair. I hadn't bought anything new for months. 'The bus station?'

'OK.'

He squeezed me to him and with a rough hand gently turned my face to his. We looked at each other and slowly, very slowly, our mouths met. His lips were dry. His tongue flicked into my mouth. 'You taste nice,' he said.

'Thank you. It's Pepsodent.

'Mmm, toothpaste, I like that.' He kissed me again, lightly. 'Got to go, girl. See you Friday.' He disappeared through the crowd as the disc jockey announced 'The One and Only, Chelmsford's biggest, most popular star, the great, the unforgettable, Georgie Fame!' People cheered and clapped and Georgie Fame bowed and ran to the electric organ and began playing *Yeah Yeah*. I stood watching, being pushed forward as the crowd surged to get a better view. I was at the front! I was standing two feet away from Georgie Fame. This was great. He looked round and smiled. I smiled back. I was feeling victorious and confident and lovely.

Still smiling I walked to the back of the hall and out into the street.

Danny was getting back into his car. Sandra stood on the steps.

Sandra said, 'Your face! The cat that got the cream!'

I tried to stop smiling. 'What did Danny say?'

'The usual. He's been let out on compassionate grounds

because his mum's not well. Or his aunty. He couldn't remember.'

'What did you say?'

'I asked him what he'd bought me for Christmas.'

'What did he say?'

'He didn't know what to choose, because I have such good taste.'

We both laughed.

'We're going shopping for something next week,' she said. 'If he turns up.'

'Will that be all right?'

'Yeah,' she said. She was being cool. It wasn't all right.

A car went past and hooted. It was a dark green Jaguar. Charlie was in the passenger seat. We both waved. 'He's going up West,' I said. 'I bet he meets someone fantastic up there who can really dance and I'll never see him again.'

'He's met you tonight, and we both know you can dance. You'll be all right. Come on, it's Christmas Eve. Everything goes right on Christmas Eve. I know that Danny's going to buy me a really expensive present and it's going to be just what I've always wanted.'

She was right. It was Christmas Eve. Tonight, I knew I'd see Charlie next Friday.

'Shall we go inside?' Sandra said. 'I haven't kissed enough people yet.' We both laughed. She linked her arm through mine and we climbed back up the steps.

The Christmas Traffic Jam

Reluctantly, they were driving to the Whites for a Christmas Eve party.

From Writtle they turned on to the A12, listening to the radio, joining in the carols.

The traffic was terrible. At Ingatestone they slowed. At Shenfield they stopped, stuck in the outside lane.

The radio said all roads into London were jammed.

After an hour someone tapped on the window. 'Have a mince pie. We're from the Allegro three cars up.'

'Oh!' said Jane. 'We have Christmas cake.'

The Fiat had sausage-rolls. The Rover had whisky. They missed the Whites but had a great A12 party.

Christmas in the Lift

It was Christmas Eve. Andrea was coming back from the town with her last-minute shopping, a frozen roast chicken TV dinner, a tin of salmon, a sliced loaf, a jar of salad cream, some tangerines, and two bars of Yardley lavender soap, in case anyone turned up, although they weren't likely to.

She also had a very small, slightly damaged Christmas tree in a pot, that the man on the market had been about to pack away. He said if she took it off his hands he would throw in the few small baubles for free, which was very nice of him. It would look quite jolly, if you turned the dried branches to the wall, and it would brighten up her living room.

She lived alone, in a flat in one of the few tall buildings in Chelmsford, on the eighth floor. This was her first Christmas there. She had arrived from Cumbria a few months before, to start a job in a local bank. She had only taken the job when her prospective boss found her accommodation in a spanking new building near the centre of town. It was a nice flat, airy, light, a bit small but she didn't need much space. She'd always had the smallest room at home.

She was on her own this Christmas. Although she'd made a few friends at the bank, none were friendly enough to ask 'Can I spend Christmas with you?' And she didn't know her neighbours. She hadn't met any of them. A lot of people in the building seemed to work in London. She'd hear the front doors slam early and the whine of the lift as they came back late. In the entrance hall there were prams and pushchairs under the stairs but she never heard children playing. There was a notice board there, too, where people asked for baby-sitters or offered tomato plants or complained about the lift. And yet she rarely saw anyone, not even in the lift.

But she liked Chelmsford. There were a lot of pubs in the town, not that she went in to them, but they sounded cheerful as she walked past on her evening stroll. There were young people sitting on their motor bikes or motor scooters, outside the local cafes, preening and flirting, which always made her smile. On a Saturday the market traders were friendly and chatty, whether it was about the price of potatoes or the quality of a pair of stockings. And on a Friday lunchtime she'd go to the cattle market, and look at the sheep and the cows.

There was a Congregational church nearby where she had been a few times. People were very welcoming. She was looking forward to the Christmas Day Service. Carols were promised in the morning and a mince pie after. Then she'd come home and have her TV dinner and settle down to the Queen's Speech and a good film. Then salmon sandwiches for tea. A perfect day.

On the third floor the lift stopped and a young woman peered in. 'Are you going down?'

'Sorry, up.'

'Oh, I'll get in anyway. I'll go up and come down again. It'll take ages whatever I do.' She stepped into the lift and shivered. 'This is nice and warm.' Her coat looked worn and her legs were bare.

The lift doors slid shut and the lift moved upwards.

'I've just been to see my mum,' the girl said. 'To wish her Happy Christmas.'

'Oh,' Andrea said politely. 'You're not spending Christmas together?'

'I don't get on with my dad, well, he's my step-dad, so it's best if I'm not there at the same time as him.' She looked sad.

'Well, your mum will have been pleased to see you,' Andrea said, briskly.

'Not really. She didn't even get me a present. And I got her a hair-dryer. It was expensive. She didn't even say thank you.' She sucked in her breath as if she was going to cry.

'I'm sure your mum will have been really pleased,' Andrea said quickly, 'even if she didn't say so. A hair-dryer is a very thoughtful present.'

The girl shrugged. 'I should have just bought her some rollers and told her to stick her head out of the window to dry it all off.'

It was an attempt at humour and Andrea smiled. 'Do you live nearby?' she asked.

'Depends what you call nearby. Witham.' A small town, ten miles away.

'Did you come on the train?'

'You must be joking. I can't afford that. I hitched. What's the time?'

'Quarter past three.'

'Well, it was a short visit, so at least it shouldn't be too dark, going back.'

'It will be quite dark,' Andrea murmured. The thought of anyone, especially a single girl - how old was she? 17, 18? - hitch-hiking in the dark on Christmas Eve, made her stomach contract. 'So is there a nice Christmas waiting for you at home?' she said hopefully.

The girl snorted. 'I'm training to be a veterinary nurse. I have a room in a hostel. Most of the girls have gone home.' Her voice caught. 'I - I thought her mum would ask me to stay.' She let out a small sob. They reached the eighth floor and the doors slid open. Andrea put one foot out onto her corridor.

The girl looked at her, 'OK, bye.' A tear rolled down her face.

She couldn't leave the poor girl like this, crying, stepping onto a dark road, sobbing and vulnerable. Andrea stepped back into the lift. 'I'll come back down with you,' she said. 'I – eh – I forgot one or two things.'

The girl looked at Andrea's bulging shopping bag. 'Don't you want to drop those off first? I can hold the lift for you.' She hiccupped.

'No,' Andrea said, 'no.' The girl would disappear, she knew. 'Why don't we press the button for the third floor? You could go and see your mum again.'

Her eyes opened wide. 'Oh, I couldn't do that.'

'I'm sure if you told her you were hoping to stay, she'd be delighted.'

A small laugh gurgled in her throat. 'No, I couldn't. Steve – that's my step-father - he'll probably be home by now. I couldn't ask her if he's there.' A look of distress flitted across her face. 'I couldn't stay anyway. It was a stupid idea. He'd go mad. And she's as scared of him as I am.'

Andrea didn't know what to say. She gazed at the girl.

And then the lift lurched. Andrea slightly lost her balance and stumbled a step or two. Then it stopped. Andrea assumed they were at a floor and waited for the doors to open and for someone to step in and relieve the unbearable tension of this conversation. But the doors didn't open. No-one else joined them. Silence filled the space; the hitherto unremarkable wheezing of the lift was gone. The young woman and Andrea looked at each other.

'Is it stuck?' she said.

Andrea was hesitant to reply, not wanting it to be true. 'Maybe.'

'What do we do?'

'Wait? It might start again.'

'That's hopeful,' she said, with irony in her voice. 'I bet we'll be stuck here. On Christmas Eve. We'll be lucky to get out of here by the time the shops shut,' she said.

The silence was all enveloping.

'It's not going to start again, is it?' She sounded hopeless.

Andrea put down her bag of shopping. 'There must be an alarm button.'

The keypad was smeared with fingerprints, dull from use. But there was a button with the image of a bell. 'Shall I?' she asked.

'I don't care.' She shook her head. 'Do what you like.' She slid down the wall and sat on the floor.

Andrea pressed the button. There was a clanging, echoing, ring. It went on and on.

'Oh god!' The girl shouted through the noise. 'Good job I'm not drunk. This would do my head in.'

The jangle of the bell suddenly stopped. Silence again.

'Well, someone must have heard that,' she said.

They waited. Nothing happened.

The girl suddenly bellowed, 'Help! Help!' Andrea joined in. They leaned back against the walls of the lift, breathless. The silence seemed even more intense.

'A lot of people have gone away for Christmas,' Andrea said, doubtfully.

'Oh great! There's no-one here. We might as well settle down and wait for Easter.'

A thought struck Andrea. 'Your mum's in, isn't she?'

'She's as deaf as a post.'

'But your step-dad's coming home? Won't he notice the lift's broken?'

'He's a keep-fit idiot. He never uses the lift. He says they break.'

'How right he is.' Andrea rang the bell again. There was the loud jangling and then overwhelming silence.

'Sit down,' the girl said. 'There's nothing else to do. My name's Valerie, by the way.'

'Hello Valerie, I'm Andrea.' She took her scarf from round her neck and put it on the dirty floor of the lift. She sat down.

And almost immediately jumped up, as a faint crackly voice spoke through the keypad. 'Hello? Who's there? What's the problem?'

'Hello!' Andrea said with relief. 'We're stuck!'

'Oh dear.' It was a man's voice. 'Sorry to hear that.'

'And we're sorry too,' Valerie shouted.

'Where are you?'

Andrea gave him the address.

She thought he said, 'Oh fuck.'

'Where are you?' she asked. 'How long will it take you to get here?'

'Well, I'm in Basildon. Oh dear …' The volume of his voice was fading and returning. 'I don't know if I'll be able to get anyone over to you tonight.'

'What!' Andrea cried. 'It's only half past three.'

'Sorry?'

She raised her voice. 'It's half past three on Christmas Eve and there are two of us stuck in this lift. You have to get us out. Tomorrow is Christmas Day!'

Behind her Valerie was snickering quietly.

'I know,' he said, his voice disappearing and returning, the crackling always there. 'I was just about to knock off when you called.'

'You can't knock off!' Andrea shrieked. 'You have to do something.'

She felt rather than heard his sigh. 'We've all got Christmas shopping to do,' he said.

'You should have done it earlier,' she shouted. 'There won't be a Christmas for us if you don't do something.'

'You should probably keep calm,' he said. 'We don't

know how long it's going to be. You don't want to use up the oxygen.'

'What!'

'I'll see what I can do,' he said. 'Don't go away.' He laughed gently and there was a click and the crackling stopped.

Andrea turned back to Valerie, trying to keep calm, trying not to use up precious air.

Valerie looked at her. 'If the worst comes to the worst, I just noticed a kind of trap door.' She pointed to the ceiling. 'We could probably poke it open if we have to. Get out that way.'

Andrea looked up doubtfully. The ceiling was high. Neither of them was tall. They had no poles or sticks. They wouldn't even be able to open it, let alone climb out.

Valerie watched Andrea's face. 'We should probably just keep still and wait,' she said.

'Yes.' Andrea clenched her fists at her side.

Valerie was taking off her coat. 'Might as well get comfortable.' She laid the coat on the floor. It was so thin, but Andrea said nothing, and they both sat down. After a moment Valerie said, 'We might have to stay for a really long time, we should sort out a toilet and stuff.'

'Oh no,' Andrea groaned.

'You've got a pot there, haven't you?' She pointed at

Andrea's heap of shopping. 'We could take the tree out and use that.'

Andrea gasped.

'But I don't need to go yet – do you?' She spoke almost tenderly. Andrea shook her head. 'We could put it over there in the corner and enjoy the decorations.'

Andrea gave her the tree. She put it under the keypad and turned the pot from side to side. 'Someone sold you a pup – it's all dead here.'

'Turn that part to the wall,' Andrea said.

Valerie stepped back and looked at the tree. 'Hmm, not bad. It's quite Christmassy, isn't it? What do you think?'

'Well, it's not quite where I expected to put it,' Andrea said, 'but it's very pretty.'

Valerie sat down again.

Andrea rummaged in her bag. 'Tangerine?'

They shared it – Valerie said sensibly that they didn't know how long their provisions would have to last – and they told each other stories of their early lives. Valerie had been to a large modern school in the centre of Colchester, and Andrea had been to a village primary school near Kendal, with only two classes. Andrea was a few years older but they had both taken the Eleven Plus exam and they had both failed. Valerie said it didn't matter as she would never have been able to go to the grammar school anyway, what with the cost of the uniform, but Andrea had always felt cheated of a proper education and had gone to night school and got some exams. Valerie was learning on the job. She had a boyfriend who was a merchant seaman who would be in Buenos Aires about now, she said. She showed Andrea his photo. He was smiling and tanned and had nice muscly arms. Valerie looked at Andrea's left hand. There was no ring there. Valerie didn't ask, but Andrea told her anyway. There had been a boy, she'd thought it was serious, but he didn't. He said he wanted to meet a few more people before he settled down. Andrea waited for him to come back, too long probably, but then she heard he was in Australia, married, a couple of kiddies.

'Oh men!' said Valerie. 'Let's have another tangerine. If that's OK.'

Two hours later they were still there.

The keypad crackled and the lift-man's voice came through. 'Hello, it's Bob again.' Andrea sprang up and went over to the keypad. 'I'm trying my best,' he said. 'I don't know how long it's going to take. Can I have your names please, and your next of kin.'

'Next of kin?' Now Valerie was on her feet. 'We're not intending to die in here.'

'Sorry, bad choice of phrase,' he mumbled. 'I just thought I could contact your nearest and dearest and they could keep trying if I have to go.'

They gave him their names and Andrea thought about her mum in her old people's home in Carlisle and how pointless it would be to ask her to organise a rescue party. It would worry her and she would think about it for hours. But Valerie poured out a list of names, including her mum's. 'She hasn't got a phone though,' she added sadly.

'All right, this is good. I'll see what I can do. Stay calm,' said Bob and he and the crackling disappeared.

'What's the time?' Valerie asked.

'Seven o'clock.'

'Seven o'clock on Christmas Eve,' Valerie groaned. 'No-one will be around to do anything useful. Don't people use the lift in this building?'

'I think the people who work in London came home at dinner time,' Andrea said. 'People usually have a short day on Christmas Eve. And a lot of people have gone away.' The pushchairs under the stairs had disappeared, she'd noticed, when she went out to the shops.

'And I'm starving,' Valerie said. 'I haven't had anything to eat since breakfast. What I could do with right now is a Christmas dinner. Wouldn't it be lovely?' She closed her eyes. 'A big bit of chicken thigh with crispy skin, some roast potatoes, no brussels of course, but loads and loads of gravy.'

Andrea was hungry herself. 'We could have a salmon sandwich,' she said.

Valerie laughed and opened her eyes. 'That's funny because a salmon sandwich is my next favourite thing at Christmas. We always have it for tea.' A mournful look came over her face. 'I could just do with a salmon sandwich.' She closed her eyes again. 'Mmm, lovely soft white bread, thick creamy butter and piles and piles of salmon. Excuse me while I take a big mouthful. Mmm mmm.' She smiled and opened her eyes. 'That was delicious. All right. You go. What do you want to eat?'

'Well, all sorts of things, but I do actually have some bread and a tin of salmon.'

'You don't!'

Andrea rummaged in her bag and pulled out the tin. 'And it's got its own key to open it with.'

'And I've got a penknife,' Valerie said.

Andrea was taken aback. She hadn't realised Valerie was the sort of person who would carry a knife.

'I'm a vet's assistant,' Valerie said. 'It's in case I need to take stones out of horses' hooves.' Andrea still looked concerned. 'And it's clean, because I never have done.'

Andrea opened the tin of salmon and took four slices of bread from the loaf. She reached into the bag again and pulled out the jar of salad cream.

'Salad cream!' Valerie exclaimed. 'This is better and

better.' She watched Andrea making the sandwiches. 'I'm glad we're locked in the lift. I'd never have had a salmon sandwich this Christmas otherwise.'

They ate their sandwiches and Valerie kept smiling. 'This is so Christmassy,' she said with her mouth full. 'Especially with the tree.' She nodded over at the pot in the corner. 'At least we haven't had to use any other purpose.'

'So far,' Andrea said darkly.

'Oh, don't say that!' Valerie said.

They laughed.

After the sandwiches they each had another tangerine.

'This is lovely.' Valerie sighed with pleasure. 'You know, we should really be singing Christmas songs.'

'Oh, let's not spoil a pleasant afternoon,' Andrea said.

'All I want for Christmas is a salmon sandwich and a tangerine,' Valerie warbled.

Andrea groaned.

'And that's what I've had,' Valerie said. 'Thank you very much.'

There was a shout outside the lift. 'Why isn't the lift working?'

Valerie and Andrea looked at each other with delight. Andrea shouted back, 'It's stuck. We're stuck. We're inside.'

'Save us!' Valerie called and laughed.

'Really?' The man's voice was surprised, almost disbelieving.

'We've been here for four hours,' Andrea shouted. 'The lift people have gone home for Christmas.'

'I'll call the fire brigade!' the man said.

Andrea shouted 'Yes, do!' And Valerie yelled. 'Please! I don't feel very well.'

Andrea looked at her. Valerie shook her head and whispered, 'You've got to say something dramatic or they won't come.'

'I think being stuck in a lift is quite dramatic,' Andrea murmured.

'OK, I'll see what I can do,' the man called.

There was silence. Andrea folded away the remains of the loaf of bread, and the tangerine peel.

'Do you think he's rung them?' Valerie said after 5 minutes.

'I'm sure he has.'

There was a shout. 'They're on their way. Sorry about that, I had to go out to the phone box.'

There was a distant jangling of a fire engine bell, then from below the sound of voices and another man's voice calling, 'Is anyone there?'

'Yes!' they shouted. 'We're here!'

'We'll have you out in a jiffy, girls! Don't panic.' There was the sound of orders being given, 'Go here,' 'Go there,' 'Fetch that!'

'Suddenly I really want to go to the toilet,' Valerie whispered.

'Hold on,' Andrea said.

And then the lift jolted. Instinctively Andrea grabbed Valerie's arm, and Valerie took her hand. The lift was moving. Slowly, grindingly, it creaked its way down. At the ground floor the doors opened and they were greeted by two firemen in navy blue uniforms. Their shining brass helmets lay on the ground beside them. 'All right, girls?' one said.

'This is better than seeing Father Christmas,' Valerie said.

'Thank you,' Andrea said. 'Particularly as it's Christmas Eve.'

'No worries,' the older man said. 'It's something for us to tell the kids.' Two more firemen in uniform appeared, coming down the stairs. 'The lift will be out of use for the next couple of days, I'm afraid.'

From inside the lift a tinny voice was calling through the key panel, 'Hello? Hello? Valerie? Andrea? Are you there?'

'We're here,' Andrea shouted.

'Can you hold on a bit longer?'

'They've held on long enough. It's all done,' the fireman called. 'No thanks to your company. There will be a report.'

'Oh! Oh, well... happy Christmas one and all.' Bob's

tinny voice disappeared.

'Now, are you all right from here on, girls? Do you live here?' the fireman asked. He looked at the scraggy Christmas tree in Andrea's arms.

'Yes.'

'No.' They spoke together.

'Can we take you anywhere?' the fireman asked.

'Well, I live in...' Valerie began.

'No,' Andrea said. 'We're all right. We're going to have a very nice Christmas upstairs.'

Valerie frowned at her. The firemen were tidying their large metal pieces of equipment. Andrea said, 'We're going to knock on your mum's front door, and if she tells you "no, there's no room at the inn," you can come and have Christmas with me. I've only got one TV dinner but we can pad it out with more potatoes.'

Valerie hesitated. 'If you're sure.'

'I'm sure.'

Valerie gave her a beaming smile. 'And there's some salmon left too, isn't there? What a fab Christmas!'

The Christmas Cracker

It was the Crompton's Christmas lunch. Cups of tea and glasses of orange sat on the table while a surreptitious bottle of whisky circulated for those who wanted it.

Roger had wangled things so he could sit beside Elaine. They had been out a couple of times, but nothing serious. He took a swig of whisky before he sat down. Everyone was pulling Christmas Crackers. When he and Elaine pulled theirs, a small plastic ring fell out. Blushing, he handed it to her.

She raised her eyebrows. 'I thought you'd never ask,' she said and slid it onto her finger.

Christmas in Paris

1961

I

It was Sylvie's first Christmas in Paris. She didn't know whether to be happy or homesick. The Christmas window displays were pretty, seemed prettier than she remembered in Chelmsford. Here the windows were all full of glittering delightful things that anyone would want to receive, pens, bags, bangles, even books looked alluring. Patisseries were filled with strange new cakes and pastries that smelled of marzipan and glistened with butter. There were swirls of snow in the air and people walked through the streets, in elegant coats, with luxurious scarves wrapped round their faces against the wind. By the hot chestnut stand on Boulevard Saint Germain people hovered, warming their hands over the glowing coals, before carrying on. In the cafés and in the kiosks, signs went up advertising *vin chaud,* hot wine with cinnamon and sometimes cloves mixed in.

More nuns than usual were going in and out of the religious shops around Saint Sulpice, as if the church was sending out its own version of Santa's helpers, to remind the people of Paris that this was a religious holiday.

Sylvie had been working in l'Etoile, for three months. L'Etoile was a bar restaurant in the genteel 7th arrondissement of Paris, frequented by the men who worked importantly in the government buildings and their overseas visitors and the film makers and actors from the old Orsay rail station.

When the boss pinned the Christmas work rota to the wall in the small staff lobby, Sylvie was dismayed to see she would be working on Christmas Eve and on Christmas Day. She looked glumly at her work colleague, Charlotte, whose name appeared in the same places. But Charlotte said, 'We might as well. What else are we going to do? Sit at home feeling gloomy? This way we get to share the fun, we'll probably get a shed load of Christmas tips, and everyone will be cheerful and they won't care if the service is slow.' Charlotte was the first friend Sylvie had made in Paris and her optimistic outlook on life was something Sylvie appreciated.

Even their boss, Remy, normally a silent, dour character, seemed to catch the Christmas spirit. The week before the big day he suggested they put small vases of Christmas roses on the table, from the florist along the street, and in the evening stubby, flickering candles, to create a Christmas glow.

Christmas Eve was the most important culinary night of the season, and that morning Remy staggered into the restaurant carrying a large box. In the lobby, he gently placed the box onto the wooden bench. Carefully he prised open the lid, removed handfuls of straw and then brought out the most exquisite plates, dishes and tureens, decorated in intricate patterns of black and gold. He said the crockery was a hundred years old, that his great grandfather had brought it all back from the Crimean War. That seemed impossible to believe – Charlotte and Sylvie exchanged a look as he delved deeper into the box - but when he drew out a large gold platter Sylvie noticed strange writing on the back. 'Cyrillic' said Charlotte knowledgeably, so perhaps it was true.

Charlotte and Sylvie were given the task of washing the plates in preparation for the evening's festivities. Periodically Remy came into the kitchen and checked that they were handling everything with care and storing them safely on a high shelf. 'One hundred years old!' he repeated.

At 6 o'clock the evening began. Men dressed in dinner jackets and women in fur coats and sparkling dresses slid happily into the room. Everyone seemed to be ordering champagne. People without reservations were asked to squeeze onto stools at the bar. Soon latecomers were told there simply was no more room.

Outside snow was falling softly, and in l'Etoile there was a warm, cheerful atmosphere and laughter and friendly conversation. The first course plates were cleared and service of the main course had begun. Sylvie and Charlotte looked at each other across the tables, as they carried the special plates laden with guinea fowl and bacon, and the delicate dishes of green beans and petits pois. They were both in their black shirts and skirts but Remy had surprised each of them with the gift of a pretty green glass brooch which now adorned their shoulders. Charlotte's cheeks were red and she stuck out her bottom lip and blew a blast of air up to her fringe. Sylvie smiled in agreement. She smoothed her long white apron and cut another baguette into thick, crisp rounds.

Delphine, the singer, who had once filled the Olympia and played to presidents and sheiks, but now sang at l'Etoile for the simple pleasure of it, appeared on the small stage. Maurice, her accordionist, helped her onto her seat. He began playing a cheerful tune, that Sylvie was sure she knew. It sounded like Sur le Pont d'Avignon, but jazzed up for 1961.

Delphine was smiling round at the diners, arranging her

skirts, when the nun came in. As the door opened a flurry of snow announced her arrival. Remy rushed forward, to wave the snow-covered creature back into the icy street, but as she attempted to wipe the snow from her habit he hesitated, then hurried to accommodate her, swearing softly under his breath. There was a single empty table, a forlorn setting for one, in a dark corner at the back, beside a pillar and a large Swiss cheese plant. It was one of Sylvie's tables, but one that was rarely used by customers. Remy would often sit there with the books and a carafe of red wine and calculate the day's profits. The nun crept through the restaurant, nodding vaguely to people who called out greetings, pleased that a member of the church had come in to share their Christmas celebrations. She slid into a chair as Remy hastily tidied his books away, and called sharply to Sylvie to attend to the new guest. The nun sat dripping and melting, telling a rosary, her lips moving silently.

Because the nun's habit was soaking and her veil so flattened and almost transparent, Sylvie didn't notice at first that she was crying. She approached the table, smiling, holding cutlery and a wine glass, and was dismayed when she saw the tears. She didn't know what to think when the nun ordered a brandy.

'Shock,' said Remy, as Sylvie placed the order. He pulled the cork out of the bottle. 'Brandy is good for shock. Something must have happened. Be kind to her.'

As Sylvie carried the brandy glass across the room, Sylvie noticed the nun's shoes, peeping out beneath her long heavy black tunic. They were pretty, pink shoes, with a small heel. A nun, in pink shoes. Sylvie placed the glass on the table. '*Tout va bien*?' she asked in what she hoped was a normal waitress tone. 'Is everything OK?'

The nun looked up at her with big eyes and opened her mouth. 'I – I need - ' she whispered.

But her next words were lost in a roar of noise as the door of the restaurant flew open. Larry, the American poet, and his musical friend Cisco came bowling in, laughing loudly, the collars of their thin coats turned up against the snow, their hair wet and wild. Both of them delved into the deep pocket of their coats and pulled out bags of sweets tied with red ribbon, which they handed round to the customers as they made their clumsy way through the restaurant. Sylvie couldn't think where they'd got bags of sweets. She feared they had plundered some communal treat for small children. 'They're drunk,' she thought. She felt responsible, as Larry was her friend.

Behind the bar Remy looked surprised, then angry, then resigned, when the smiles and murmurs of the patrons showed they were happy to be so interrupted.

Sylvie stood with Charlotte, squeezed at the end of the bar, waiting for Remy to open more champagne. Charlotte said simply, 'The customers think it's part of the evening.'

'Oh, but look at them,' Sylvie moaned softly. *A sobbing nun at my table and now two wet loud-mouths who are my friends*, she thought.

Larry and Cisco were sitting on the floor at Delphine's feet in front of the stage, clapping loudly and calling for her to sing. Maurice, who was Cisco's special friend, looked exasperated. But Delphine smiled indulgently at the two men. Larry lived next door to Delphine in the same 17th Century building in the Latin Quarter, so she knew him. She put her finger to her lips to quiet them and with a little harrumphing and coughing and looking round at the room, they became still. Delphine adjusted the chiffon scarf around her neck, and began to sing.

It was one of her soft, throaty, heart-breaking songs. Maurice played tenderly, harmonizing with her husky, cracked voice, and the room fell silent as if enchanted. Glasses were put aside and knives and forks laid down as everyone gazed at her. Sylvie and Charlotte moved around the tables, noiselessly removing plates and serving dishes. Then they too stood silently by, as Delphine sobbed and crooned of the love she had lost but that might one day return.

As she reached the last shuddering notes of the song, there was a crash. Sylvie spun round. The leaves on the Swiss Cheese plant were quivering, dripping with gravy. On the floor was a mess of meat and lying in the middle, triumphantly holding aloft the 100-year-old plate, was Larry, beside a furious Remy.

II

Larry staggered to his feet and with exaggerated care put the golden plate onto the table with the nun. As Remy turned to berate Larry for leaving his feet too close to the tables, the nun touched his arm and shook her head.

Delphine had heard the crash and looked across at the table with the sad nun, the dishevelled poet, the angry bar owner, and Sylvie and Charlotte speedily wiping the floor. She put her mouth close to the microphone. 'Come,' she whispered to the room, 'come. It is so cold outside, here it is so comfortable. Relax, be at your ease...' She was tapping her thigh rhythmically, while Maurice played softly in the background. 'Come,' she repeated, raising her voice, and the accordion grew louder. 'Let us all sing the song that you know so well. I could have made a million from it but I gave it to Edith Piaf,' she growled. Already the diners were singing along. It was Milord. All eyes were upon Delphine as Sylvie silently mouthed *thank-you* as she and Charlotte cleared away the spilled meat and gravy and vegetables.

'So many carrots,' Sylvie moaned. She looked up at the table where Larry was sitting, talking to the nun, their

116

heads close together.

'Do they know each other?' Charlotte murmured.

'Maybe.' Sylvie watched as the little nun began to smile. Larry was stroking the back of her hand. 'Perhaps the pink shoes should tell us something,' she said.

'Oh, well she's definitely not a nun,' Charlotte said. They walked to the back of the restaurant, into the store room, and deposited the spoiled meal into a dustbin.

'Do you know her?' Sylvie asked.

'No, but a real nun wouldn't let a man stroke her hand. Wouldn't let anyone touch her hand.'

'Who is she, then?' Sylvie said stepping back into the restaurant, but Remy was looking at them and they had to separate and deliver more champagne, and tarte tatin and plates of cheese to the red-cheeked diners.

Now that the crisis had passed Delphine changed the mood. Now she was once again softly crooning old love songs that everyone seemed to know, and if they weren't singing along, they were nodding or swaying gently. Sylvie couldn't imagine a scene like this in England. Not in a restaurant. In a pub maybe, with beer and packets of crisps and a regular old girl who just came in out of the cold every Friday and sang 'Won't You Come Home, Bill Bailey'. But not this complete sense of togetherness.

Larry and the nun had now been joined at the table by Cisco. Larry raised his hand. Sylvie could not ignore them.

As she exchanged the full ashtray for an empty clean one, Larry said, 'Could we have some red wine, Mademoiselle?' He couldn't quite sit up straight. He was tilting towards the nun.

'Mademoiselle?' repeated Sylvie. 'You're calling me Mademoiselle?'

'Would you rather I called you Madam?'

Sylvie glowered at him.

'Ah,' Larry said, 'she's acknowledging me at last! Good evening, my dear Sylvie, how are you?'

Cisco looked embarrassed. 'Have you been introduced to Mireille?' he said quickly.

'That's Sister Mireille to you,' Larry muttered.

The nun looked up at Sylvie with big eyes, still trembling with tears.

'Good evening, Mireille,' Sylvie whispered.

'Mireille has just been fired!' Larry said.

'What do you mean?' Sylvie began wiping the table, trying to look busy, in case Remy called her away.

'She was a nun,' Larry said. The nun sobbed. 'And now she isn't.'

'Can you sack nuns?' Sylvie asked, privately thinking, *I bet it was the pink shoes that did it.*

'Oh, not *that* kind of a nun,' Larry said, his head now almost on the nun's shoulders. 'She was playing a nun.'

'At the *Théâtre Chatelet*,' the nun sobbed. 'It was my

118

biggest role.'

'And... she got drunk at lunchtime.'

'I wasn't drunk,' she protested. 'I'd just had a glass of *pastis*. One drink. To celebrate Christmas.'

'And, let's face it, all nuns celebrate Christmas, don't they?' Larry slurred.

'I suppose so, in one way or another,' Sylvie murmured. She looked at Larry. 'Was she with you?'

'No! I never met the girl before tonight.'

What a fast mover you are, Sylvie thought, looking at his face so close to the nun's.

Larry blinked. 'I can see from your face that you think forcing alcohol on a poor nun is something I would do. I would not. In fact, if you want to blame anyone, blame Cisco, he's the one with musical connections.' Larry's head was tipping close to the table. His eyelids drooped.

'It was just one drink,' repeated Mireille.

Sylvie looked at Cisco.

'Mireille knows Maurice. He did some work on the show,' Cisco said. 'Careful, Sylvie, here comes trouble.'

Remy marched over to the table, breathing heavily. 'Now what is happening?' he said.

With difficulty Larry raised his head. 'Mireille has come to perform,' he slurred.

Remy looked at Sylvie. 'Why are talking to these people? Why is this nun being troubled? What is he talking about?'

'She's an actress,' Sylvie mumbled, not sure if it was true.

'And she's going to sing,' Larry said.

'Well, no-one has mentioned this to me. We shall see!' Remy was still talking to Sylvie. 'If I discover that your friends are attempting to ruin the evening of my guests, you, mademoiselle, will be taking your coat and not returning.' He turned towards the stage where Delphine had just finished a yearning love song. There were murmurs of approval from the diners, then a smattering of applause, and conversations began again. Maurice played soft, gentle interlude music, his fingers running up and down the keyboard of his accordion.

From his position by the nun's table, Remy beckoned to Delphine.

Delphine raised an eyebrow and turned to Maurice. Maurice looked across at the table. He stopped playing and stepped down from the stage. Still carrying his accordion, he walked across the room. He greeted Cisco with a kiss on each cheek, and looked down at Mireille.

'This girl has apparently come to perform!' Remy said.

Maurice frowned.

Larry sat up. 'You remember, Maurice. We talked about this with Delphine last week. Didn't we Cisco?'

Cisco nodded vaguely.

'Just a couple of numbers,' Larry said, 'nothing fancy.

You can sing *La Mer,* can't you?' He nudged Mireille.

'Yes, I can,' she said.

'There you are!' Larry sounded triumphant. 'And Delphine clearly needs a break. And Maurice will play.'

'Don't I need a break?' said Maurice.

'You are young and virile,' said Larry. His head was drooping but he kept jerking it back up.

Remy looked at Mireille. She was dryer now. 'Are you really a singer?'

She nodded.

'Do you have to wear that outfit?'

'It's all I have.' Mireille's lip trembled. 'And I can sing a song from the show, which goes with the habit. Maurice knows it.'

Maurice sighed. He went back to talk to Delphine. She listened, nodding gravely.

She held the microphone and said huskily, 'And now a little Christmas treat from the production currently playing just across the river - I'm sure you've all been to see it - *The Miracle*!' There were approving sounds from the diners. Anything Delphine said was all right with them. 'And to sing the hit song The Love of a Minstrel Boy, it is Mademoiselle Mireille Sinclair!'

Mireille stumbled over to the stage. There were murmurs of approval around the room, as if they had known all along that the nun was a celebrity. Delphine embraced Mireille and handed over the microphone. Mireille whispered 'Thank you.' Maurice began to play a low, repetitive melody. Mireille didn't move.

After a few beats she began to sing. Her voice was lighter than Delphine's, it was smooth and sweet. As Maurice ran his hands across the keys, her voice rose and swooped in a way that made shivers run up Sylvie's spine. It was a song she realised she knew. She had heard it on the radio, but never like this. As the song drew to a close, applause burst out and people shouted 'Bravo!'

Pink spots burned on Mireille's cheeks as she bowed. She turned to Delphine, still sitting at the back of the stage, and held out the microphone. Delphine stepped forward and embraced Mireille. She called to Maurice who began to play *Je ne regrette rien* and she and Mireille stood together, arms around each other, singing.

At the end of the song, amid the cheers from the diners and the whooping from Larry and a smile from Remy, the door to the restaurant opened. A young man stood uncertainly, blinking in the warmth and bright lights. Sylvie went across to him. 'I am looking for Mireille,' he stammered. 'We need her in the theatre. She is the understudy to the star. And the star is not well. Mireille must come now!'

Sylvie told the young man not to worry and wove her way quickly through the tables to the stage where she called to Mireille. Mireille bent down to hear her then rose with a beatific smile. 'This has been a wonderful evening, but I must go,' she announced, her head held high. 'I wish you all a very Happy Christmas!'

The Box of Christmas Baubles

Teddy wanted to decorate the tree. It was just a branch because there was no money, after decades of financial disasters and tall stories of missing treasure. Grandma pulled out an old, dusty box of baubles. Teddy wiped them carefully. They gleamed in the light, reflecting the small fire and the paper-chains round the room. Clumsily he hooked one onto the twig. It fell, shattered, shards of glass fell into the box. Teddy began to cry.

'It's just an old bauble,' grandma comforted him, then saw something glittering among the shards. A solid gold coin. Her father's long lost 'treasure.'

The Christmas Card

1965

The Christmas card arrived two days before Christmas. It was waiting on the telephone table in the hall when Carol came home from work. She wasn't expecting any more cards. She had sent eight and had received eight. And now this.

It was a pretty card, with a dusting of glitter, the picture itself of a cosy cottage under a starry night sky, lights glowing in the windows and the roof covered in snow. Inside the card she couldn't make out the signature. The words read, 'Have a something something Xmas with all something' and a squiggle for a name followed by three kisses.

Carol looked at the envelope. She thought she recognised the handwriting, she'd seen it before, but she couldn't remember when. It was spiky and scrawled – the handwriting of someone anxious to get their ideas down on paper, the ends of letters flying into the air. But everything was written with a fountain pen in black ink. Using a fountain pen seemed too thoughtful for this scrawly writing. And she couldn't think who she knew who used a fountain pen. She herself hadn't even dipped a pen into an inkwell since her last couple of years in primary school, always coming home with the middle finger of her right hand stained a watery navy blue.

She decided to keep the envelope as well as the card. It was a bit of a mystery and she liked that. In the days that followed she looked at the card and then the envelope with the dramatic urgent handwriting, wondering what it reminded her of, who it reminded her of. She stood the card up on her window sill with the other cards, from her aunts and her nan and from Angie, her best friend.

That night Angie came round to listen to records on Carol's record-player, and do a final fitting for the dress that Angie was making for her for a Christmas present. As the Ronettes sang about Frostie the Snowman Angie settled onto the bed. 'Show me the card,' she said and Carol reached across to the window ledge.

Angie studied the picture. 'So who might it be?' She opened the card. 'Look at that handwriting!' she exclaimed. She held it close to her face. '"*Have a* what? What? *Xmas* something something *love*.'

'Love?' Carol snatched the card from her hand. 'It doesn't say love. Does it?'

Angie shrugged. She took back the card and read out the printed message. '*Thinking of you this Christmas time.* Who might be thinking of you?'

'You? My mum? My aunties? I don't think that helps. I've got all my cards.'

'What about people at work?'

'I don't think we send each other cards.' This was her second year in the lab at Britvic's.

'Who do we know now who might have sent it? How about people from the Orpheus?'

'People we see in a coffee bar aren't going to send me cards.'

'Show me the envelope.' Angie laid the card and envelope side by side on the bed. 'Well, that's not a girl's handwriting,' she said.

'How can you tell?'

'Well, every girl we know writes so you can read it. That's just ...'

'Illegible?'

They both looked at the card again. 'But it's such a pretty card,' Carol said. 'You'd think it was a girl who sent it.'

'He probably nicked one of his mum's.' Angie gazed at the card. She shook her head. 'I've got no idea.' She looked at her watch. 'We'd better get on with the dress, if you're going to have anything to wear on Christmas Eve.' They were going to the dance at the Corn Exchange.

Tenderly Carol put the card back in its place between the cards from Angie and her cousin Michelle, then changed into the half-finished creation that Angie had brought with her. It was a straight maroon shift with long sleeves and grey fur at the cuffs and the neck.

'Looks good,' said Angie, standing back, studying Carol with narrowed eyes.

'There was a boy at primary school who used to write like that,' Carol said, as she turned slowly while Angie pinned the hem. 'I always wanted him to be my partner when we did country dancing. But he always chose Gloria Baker.' She looked down at Angie.

'Possible,' Angie said, with pins in her mouth.

'Except he moved away just before we took the eleven plus. Oh, it's hopeless,' Carol said but then she looked at herself in the mirror on the wardrobe door and smiled. 'I love this. Christmas Eve is going to be really great.'

'Do you want me to wrap it up?' Angie asked. 'Or will you come round to mine on Saturday? We can get ready together and you can put it on then.'

Carol did a final twirl in front of the mirror, her eyes bright with pleasure. 'Oh, I'll come to yours,' she said.

With a jingle of sleigh bells, Carol's favourite girl group, The Crystals chorused 'Santa Claus is coming to town,' as Angie packed the dress away and the girls went down stairs.

Angie called goodbye to the household. 'Saturday is going to be such a good evening,' she said at the front door.

'I know!' Carol ran upstairs as Bob B Soxx crooned 'Here Comes Santa Claus'.

The little card sat on the window sill until a few days after Christmas. Carol always kept a few of her cards, this year she saved the one from her mum and dad, the card from Angie and the mystery card. After she had written the final entry of the year in her diary on the 31st December, she slid the cards between the covers, and tucked the diary away in the back of her wardrobe.

1975

It was the week before Christmas and Carol was doing some shopping in Oxford Street. To avoid the crowds, she was taking a leisurely, late lunch hour. She worked as a pharmacist in a chemist's shop on Margaret Street. They were never busy on Wednesday afternoons.

It was a cold, blustery day and she buttoned her coat as she came out of John Lewis, laden with bags. She was pleased with her purchases, confident in the gift for her mum, a turquoise and enamel bangle, unsure about the green snazzy socks for her dad and content with the generous record token for her younger brother Richard. She had also bought some pretty Christmas paper and a ball of bright red ribbon and she was looking forward to doing the wrapping tonight, while watching TV.

'Hello! It's Carol, isn't it? Carol Wakefield. Oh, my goodness!' In the street, a woman, also carrying shopping bags, also bundled up in a scarf and a warm coat, was gazing at her.

Carol hesitated, not wanting to be rude.

'It's Gloria. Gloria Robson, well, Baker that was. From school.'

'Gloria! I would never have recognised you.' She had blond hair now, hanging loose to her shoulders; she had a smooth skin and turquoise eye shadow. 'How did you know it was me?'

'That lovely brown hair of yours and your eyes. I always envied your eyes'

'Did you?'

'I was so pleased we were best friends.'

'We were...?' Carol began slowly.

'Oh, don't you remember, we were always laughing in country dancing. Mrs Greer was always trying to get the boys to dance with us.'

'Was she?'

And you helped me with my arithmetic.'

'Did I?'

'Oh, I can't believe we've bumped into each other like this. This is lovely. I'm just about to go and have a cup of tea.' She lifted her bags. Carol noticed they were very nice carrier bags. 'I'm exhausted! Come with me!'

Carol was trying to organise her thoughts. Gloria. For years she had thought of her – if she had thought of her at all – as an enemy, a rival, rather than a friend. She looked at her watch. She had a few minutes. She'd finished her shopping. Gloria pulled open the door of John Lewis and Carol followed her in and they went up to the café.

The lunchtime rush was over and they found a quiet table. Carol was hanging her coat over the seat when a man with a red face, wearing a tight overcoat, approached.

He looked surprised. 'Hello!' He looked from Gloria to Carol and back.

'This is my husband,' Gloria said. 'Roger. Roger, this is Carol. Bur of course, you must remember her. We were all at school together.'

'Of course. Carol.' He shook his head. He sat down. He leaned towards Gloria and pecked her on the cheek. 'God I'm starving. Where's the menu?'

Carol was embarrassed. 'I'm sorry – I didn't mean to intrude on your lunch plans. I really should be getting back to work.'

'No, no,' said Gloria. 'We have a lot to say, don't go yet.' She waved her hand dismissively towards Roger. 'He can have a sandwich.'

'No, I must go.' She began to struggle into her coat.

'Oh, but we can't lose touch now. Roger, write our address down for her. You must come and see us.'

'Give me something to write on,' he said.

Gloria rummaged in her bag. She pulled out a used envelope. Roger pulled a fountain pen from the breast pocket of his suit, and unscrewed the lid. He pushed his plate to one side and on the back of the envelope, wrote down an address.

He gave the envelope to Carol. She noted the address. Springfield.

'Yes, we're still in Chelmsford,' Gloria said. 'Where do you live?'

'I –I live in London, West - West Hampstead.' She was looking at the envelope.

'That's nice. Are you married?'

'No, no, I've got – I've got a flat.' She turned the envelope over and looked at the Christmas stamp.

'Oh, of course,' Gloria said, 'I could have just given you the envelope. It's already got our address on. So that's us, right there.'

Carol was staring hard at the envelope. The handwriting. It was the handwriting. That spiky, urgent handwriting that she remembered so well. It wasn't Roger's handwriting. She was looking at the front of the envelope. She looked up at Gloria and back at the envelope.

'Well, now you have our address twice, so you really

134

must come and see us.'

'But who, who sent you this – this envelope?'

Gloria took it from her and studied the writing.

'That's a good question. Who was it from, Roger?'

'Oh, don't ask me,' he said. He was trying to catch the attention of the waitress. 'Wasn't it just a flyer? An advert or something?'

Gloria stared at the envelope. 'Hmm. Perhaps you're right. Let me think ... I think it was from the butcher's. Our old butcher's on the Broomfield Road. I don't know why. We never shop there anymore. We've got a very nice butcher in Springfield. Everything's always very fresh.'

Carol laughed, a happy gurgling in her throat. She waved the envelope. 'You got this, this year?'

'Yes,' said Gloria. 'What's funny? A good butcher is hard to find.'

'Oh, I'm sure that's true,' Carol said. 'Very true. Well, thank you. I'll definitely keep this.'

That night she rang home for the weekly phone call with her mum. They discussed the arrangements for Carol's Christmas visit. Her mum said, 'And you don't need to bring home any of that salami you like. We can buy it in Chelmsford now. They do it in the butcher's.'

'Which butcher's?'

'Which one do you think? The butcher's on the parade.

They've taken over the shop next door, and they've made that into – what do they call it – a delicatessen. Lots of things with garlic. Salami and everything.'

'Gosh.' Carol laughed. 'Do you remember Alec who used to work there?'

'Was that the boy you were always talking about?'

'I wasn't.'

'So you say. But, yes, he's still there. He's the owner now. It was his idea to open a delicatessen. And apparently it's going very well. I told him you were coming home.'

'You didn't.'

'He sent his love.'

Carol laughed. 'He didn't.'

Going back to Chelmsford on the train, she wondered about him. She wondered if he still had his motorbike and his leather jacket. Or had she imagined the leather jacket? She couldn't stop smiling. At the bus station she boarded a 43 that was just about to leave. She paid to go as far as the Parade. She wasn't sure if the shop would still be open at this time. It used to close at 5. It was twenty-to now. Well, she told herself, whatever happened, the walk home would do her good.

She got off the bus and stood for a moment, looking at the row of shops that had always seemed so exotic and exciting. There was a light dusting of snow in the air and a group of carol singers, with woollen hats and thick scarves, were standing in front of the shops, singing *I saw three ships go sailing by*. The Clock House pub, the bakers, the post office, and there the butcher's and right next door to it the new delicatessen, all were decorated with Christmas garlands, red and gold in every window.

She walked into the butchers. It smelled the same, sawdust and meat, but the kiosk had gone. There were Christmas decorations – fairy lights looped round the walls. The Merry Christmas sign now stuck above the new decimalised cash register, and the pig was still there, with a wreath of holly round its neck. There was a boy in a white coat, with spiky hair, talking earnestly to an old lady, telling her how long she needed to cook her small chicken.

And then, from the store room at the back, in came Alec, carrying a large ham. He went over to a woman in a fur coat, and Carol watched him, chatting and smiling, as he sliced the meat, and wrapped the meat, occasionally looking over at the boy and nodding agreement with his suggestions. There was not so much grease in his hair now, Carol noticed, but still there was a lock falling across his forehead.

The woman in the fur coat paid and turned to go and Carol stepped forward. A blast of cold air blew in as the woman opened the door, but she held it open, and looked back, saying, 'And the sausage meat is in the bag too?'

'Yes, it's all there,' Alec said cheerfully. 'You'll have a very happy Christmas with that lot on the table.'

She smiled at him, a big smile with a lot of lipstick. Carol watched her with a tremor of uncertainty.

'Yes madam?' Alec was looking at her. And then really looking at her.

She smiled at him.

'Well, hello,' he said. 'It's our very own Christmas Carol.'

'The very same.' She grinned.

The old lady was making her way to the door. 'Happy Christmas everyone,' she called. The boy darted forward and opened the door for her.

Alec was standing, gazing at Carol, shaking his head. He looked at his watch. 'We close in 5 minutes. Can you stay?'

'Well, I...'

'Oh, I'm sorry.' A flush coloured his cheeks. 'Have you come to buy something?'

'No.' She shook her head. 'I – I came to see you. If you're free.'

A smile flickered across his lips. 'I'm free.' He coughed. 'We could go to the Clock House for a Christmas drink.'

'I'd like that,' she said. 'You can tell me about your delicatessen and what you've been doing for the last 10 years, since you sent me that Christmas card.'

'You got it then?'

'Yes, but I couldn't read your writing.'

'So *that* was why you never came to the Compasses.'

'Oh well, that's another story,' she said.

He laughed.

The boy, who was sweeping the floor, stared at the two of them.

Alec glanced at his watch again. 'Rory, you get off home. I'll close up.' Rory looked gratefully at Carol and took off his stained white coat.

Alec pulled down the blinds and took off his own coat. 'Excuse me.' He held up his hands. 'I have to wash.' He disappeared into the back room.

She was alone in the shop. He had turned off the main light and now the room was lit with just the fairy lights. The faint sound of the carol singers came through the door. Alec came back into the room, sweeping his hair back with his hand.

'Do they have mistletoe in the Clock House?' she said.

'I – I really don't know. Why do you ask?'

She wished she had had a glass of sherry before she arrived. She needed courage to find out what was going to happen. What he would say to her? She couldn't bear to sit in the Clock House if he was going to tell her about his wife and two kids. 'Last time I was here you gave me a Christmas kiss.'

'That was different,' he said. 'I was young then.'

Her heart sank.

'Because,' he went on, 'when I kissed you then, I kissed you on the cheek.' He stepped forward and took her face in both hands. 'Is it all right if I kiss you on the mouth?'

She nodded. He kissed her. And it was soft and deep and lovely.

Waiting for a Christmas Kiss

She had been waiting for his return for two years. This and that meant he hadn't come home. She decorated the tree, bought a chicken, made a cake.

The family came, stayed the night, then staggered down to lunch. They pulled crackers, put on hats, read out the jokes. She switched on the telly – the youngsters liked Top of the Pops.

When the doorbell rang, they looked at each other.

She opened the door and there he was, all six foot of him, in his uniform, kit-bag on his shoulder. 'Hello ma,' he said and bent down and kissed her.

The Christmas Meal

Marie opened the front door, when Bill and his family arrived, because Bill was her fiancé and that's how you did things.

Bill gave her a peck on the cheek and a small box wrapped in gaudy red and green paper. She hoped it was the earrings she had taken so much trouble to point out to him in the window of Walkers, the jewellers in the High Street. 'Put that under the tree,' he muttered. 'It's for Wendy.'

She didn't understand and looked down at the box and up at his face, as his mum and dad, and his sister Diane, stepped into the hall, unbuttoning their coats. Mr Carter talked about the traffic-free roads, and what a good run it had been, Mrs Carter called a general hello, and then in came an unknown, pretty girl, in old-fashioned winkle-picker shoes, tossing a shiny head of blonde curls.

'Oh yes,' Mrs Carter whispered to Marie, 'this is Wendy.'

'*Who's Wendy*?' Marie wanted to say. She knew there would be more than one answer to that question. Who she was in real life being one, and who she was in relation to

Bill being another. Bill was helping Wendy out of her coat, laughing softly as his hand accidentally brushed her breast.

'Wendy's Diane's pen-friend from Manchester,' Mrs Carter said, as Mr Carter peered at the barometer that hung on the wall above the telephone table. He tapped the glass. 'Well, at least it's not going to rain.'

'But you look very nice, Marie,' Mrs Carter said. 'I don't know how you keep so thin.'

'It's because she knows I like my girls skinny,' Bill said.

'Oh Bill,' said Mrs Carter.

'You'd better go into the front room,' Marie said, weighed down with coats now. From Wendy's coat, the top of the pile, rose a sweet smell of perfume.

'They're *here*,' Marie called over her shoulder towards the kitchen where Mrs Brady was preparing the meal.

Mrs Brady red and harassed came into the hall. 'You took your time!' she said. 'Who's this?' She looked at Wendy who was giggling at something that Bill had been whispering to her.

'This is Diane's penfriend,' Marie said shortly.

'Oh. Marie, take those coats upstairs and get Sandra down here, now. She'll have to go next door and get another tin of peas. Where's Fred?'

'Dad's in the shed,' Marie said, toiling up the stairs. She felt close to tears.

'Hope you don't mind,' Mrs Carter explained. 'Wendy's

got an interview in London the day after Boxing Day and it's easier for her if she starts off from Chelmsford rather than Manchester.'

'Salford,' Wendy said.

'She speaks!' said Bill.

They all went into the front room and someone shut the door, so Marie couldn't hear anymore as she toiled upstairs with the coats.

Sandra came out of the bathroom. She had obviously been experimenting with the new lipstick she had given herself for Christmas. It was orange and made her look ill, or perhaps that was just how Marie felt. 'Get downstairs,' Marie hissed. 'They're all here. There's some girl who says she's Diane's penfriend.'

Sandra leaned over the bannisters. 'Where?'

'They're in the front room.'

'I didn't know Diane had a penfriend.'

'You don't know everything.'

'Did you know she had a penfriend?'

'That's not the point.'

'She's probably Bill's bit on the side,' Sandra said. 'He's got a nerve.'

'Shut up!' Marie threw the coats on Sandra's bed. 'He wouldn't dare.'

'You know Bill,' Sandra trilled.

Marie did know Bill. 'You'd better go downstairs quick, you've got to go next door and ask Mrs Raymond for another tin of peas.'

'Why have I got to go?'

'Because he's my fiancé and they're his family and I have to stay in the same house as them.' She looked at herself in the mirror to see how he would see her.

'You'd better get down there yourself,' Sandra said. 'Before he stands under the mistletoe with Miss Penfriend.'

'Her name's Wendy,' Marie hissed as she flew down the stairs.

Before she could go into the front room Mrs Brady called her in to the kitchen to lay an extra place at the table. 'You'll have to sit on the stool from the shed,' Mrs Brady said. 'It's your fault she's here.'

'My fault.'

'If you weren't engaged to him, she wouldn't be here.'

If I wasn't engaged to him, I wouldn't be here, she thought.

'Everyone can sit up now,' Mrs Brady called, and they jostled in to the small alcove off the kitchen that at Christmas they called the dining room. Everyone was rosy and cheerful from the Irish whisky Mr Brady had served in the best small glasses with the shamrocks on.

'Where shall I sit?' Wendy said.

'You can sit on the stool,' Sandra said.

'And you can shut up,' Bill said. 'She'll sit here next to me.'

Mrs Brady carried in the full plates and placed them on the table, Mr and Mrs Carter first, then Bill and Wendy, and after that Diane and Mr Brady, then Sandra and Marie and lastly herself.

'I don't like peas,' Wendy said, looking worriedly at her plate. 'We don't have them like this in our house.'

'Well, we have them like this in *our* house,' Sandra said loudly and Marie was pleased, even though the peas Mrs Raymond had given Sandra were not the ones the family usually had and the mix of processed and garden peas was unusual.

Marie loved Christmas dinner. She loved the chicken and the gravy and the mashed potato, all served on the best plates with the tiny delicate flowers round the edge that only came out for special occasions like Christmas and her mum and dad's wedding anniversary. She loved sitting in the room with the Christmas lights and everyone being jolly and telling cracker jokes. What do you call a cross between a reindeer and a bicycle? She couldn't remember the answer for laughing. But that was last year. Last year before she got engaged to Bill. Bill hadn't come to Christmas dinner last year, he came up in the afternoon and they had snuggled on the settee and watched television, eating chocolates.

This year it all felt so different. The food was the same,

the plates were the same, but Bill was looking at the food on her plate, murmuring, 'Fatso.' And the lights had fused and hung limp and dark, and now the effect of the whisky had worn off and no-one was being jolly. Except Bill and Wendy. Marie could tell he was either tickling Wendy or touching her leg because she kept whispering at him to stop, giggling and red in the face. And Wendy got the sixpence from the Christmas pudding. Sandra got the threepenny joey. Normally Marie and Sandra got one each, but not this year. Even Bill complained. He felt the girls were ganging up on the boys and why hadn't he won something? She tried to catch his eye, to give him a sympathetic look, to say they were in the same boat, but he didn't look at her.

Afterwards there were presents. They sat in the front room, Wendy on the settee next to Bill, Mr and Mrs Carter on the two armchairs. Mr and Mrs Brady silently on two hard dining room chairs. Marie sat on the pouffe next to the electric piano, with Sandra beside her on the floor, the nearest person to the tree, picking up the packages, examining the labels, calling people's names.

When half of the presents had been handed out, Sandra yawned and turned to her own gifts. She unwrapped the offering from Marie. It was two lucky charms for her bracelet – a tiny lipstick and a horse-shoe – which Marie was confident Sandra wouldn't like and which she would be able to claim back in a week or so. But the pleasure for that small victory was eclipsed by the sight of Wendy holding the gift which she, Marie, had herself put under the tree. 'That's from me, by the way,' Bill said loudly, amid the rustle and the ripping of paper.

Beneath hooded lids Marie watched Wendy's eager fingers as she scrabbled at the wrapping on the box. She shuddered at Wendy's small cries of pleasure and mock frustration with the impossibility of undoing the bow. Bill never put a bow on presents to Marie. His gift to her still sat under the tree. She had seen Bill slide it there just before they sat down for dinner. It was another small box. Whatever it was, it had to be jewellery. Bill always gave her jewellery. It was their thing. Like 'Love me tender' was their song. And 'The Nun's Story' was their film – because that was the first film they had ever seen together, sitting upstairs in the back row of the Regent, the really expensive seats. She reached for the box now, Bill's gift, her fiancé's gift, to her, his fiancée. She tucked the box into the palm of her hand and was comforted by it. It would be something nice, something different, that would make people say 'Gosh!' because that was Bill's way. She would open it when everyone else had finished and then people would be impressed and Wendy, who couldn't even unwrap a present, would see the way things were.

After a suggestion from Bill, Mrs Brady gave Wendy some scissors, and she snipped through the ribbon and tore off the paper. The room was suddenly still as she eased off the lid.

It was earrings. Not the earrings that Marie had wanted. No, not those, but the more expensive ones that had been in the tray, next to the pair Marie had pointed out. The more expensive ones that they had looked at in the window, when Bill had said immediately, 'Don't think you're getting them ones. You think I'm made of money?' And she had pointed out the smaller, quieter, cheaper pair as the ones she really liked.

'Oh but I haven't got pierced ears,' Wendy was saying anxiously to Diane.

'Anyone got a needle?' Sandra shouted. 'I'll do it.'

'My mum would go mad,' Wendy said. 'I mean, they're lovely, but I can't.' She shook her head. 'Does anybody want them?' Limply she held out the box.

Marie was astounded. She looked at Bill. His face was white. She knew what that meant. He was cross, very cross. 'I'll have them,' she said.

But Bill had bounded from his seat and snatched the box from Wendy's hand. 'It's all right. It was just a joke. I need to take them back to the shop.'

They all stared at him.

'Anyway I've got to go now.' His body was rigid with anger.

Mrs Brady said, 'But there's the tea to come. I got that

salmon you like.' She'd ordered it in specially in the shop. Mr Roberts, the owner, thought she'd gone mad. 'Do you want a sherry, then?' She was anxious.

Marie wanted to shout at Bill. He was spoiling it all. For everyone. If he was going to be like this he shouldn't have come.

'No, I'm going,' he said. 'I've got to see a bloke in town.'

Now his mum was frowning. 'But what about the cake? I've made the cake.'

'Bring it home. I'll have some then.'

He strode out of the room. In the silence the front door slammed.

'More salmon for us then,' Sandra said. She didn't even like salmon. But she liked Bill less.

Wendy said, 'Shall we play a game?'

'Such as...?' Sandra said. They didn't normally play games.

'How about charades?'

Bill's mum said, 'Oh, I say. That sounds fun.'

Diane turned to her. 'Mum, he's gone now. You don't have to keep trying to enjoy yourself.'

'Now he's gone we can all enjoy ourselves,' said Sandra.

'Sandra! Don't be bold,' said Mr Brady.

'Shall I start?' Wendy rose and stood in front of the electric fire.

Marie explained the rules to her mum and dad, and

soon they were all shouting, trying to guess what Wendy was miming.

When Mr Brady successfully acted out The Rover's Return, they all laughed and agreed it was a very good game, and now they were ready for their tea.

Marie realised she hadn't thought about Bill for over an hour. She was so hungry she had two slices of cake.

The Christmas Revelation

The room was warm, fairy-lights glinting, the Christmas tree shimmering with baubles.

Ellen sat alone, as she did every Christmas, a glass of red wine in front of her, her cheeks rosy, hair a little astray. This place had memories. She had been coming here for 20 years, on Christmas Eve. The first time had been Christmas Day when the café was shut.

A stranger stepped forward. Ellen had never seen her before but there was something in her eyes, the tilt of her lips.

'I was left on the step outside this café on Christmas Day 20 years ago.'

The Christmas Day Dinner Disaster

The Christmas dinner was in the oven. The rich, unusual smell of cooking chicken filled the house along with the sound of the sizzling fat crisping the skin. The roast potatoes were about to go in to the oven. Carol and her mum were in the kitchen, both with red faces, peeling brussel sprouts. Occasionally Carol had to look into the steamer where the Christmas pudding in a glass bowl with a greaseproof paper lid tied with string was slowly steaming to perfection. Carol's job was to keep the bottom pan topped up with water.

Earlier a precious bottle of milk had slipped from Carol's hands and smashed in the hall. It was a calamity. There had been tears and despair. Now Mr Hart had gone out to see if he could find a shop that would sell milk today. He wasn't having much luck. The custard for the Christmas pudding would have to be made with two tins of evaporated milk which Mrs Hart said would do just as well, if not better.

In the living room Richard was playing Monopoly, his longed-for Christmas present, with Lady, the family cocker spaniel. His best friend Malcolm who lived next door was not allowed to play out on Christmas day, and Carol had point blank refused to play with him, so it had to be Lady. He helped her by throwing the dice and making some of the difficult decisions for her, and Lady had won Liverpool Street and the Old Kent Road but was not playing with the enthusiasm Richard had hoped for. Although she was panting as if she was very excited about the game and couldn't wait for the next throw of the dice, she also kept getting up and walking round the room.

Carol went to lay the table in the front room. She took the clean white cotton cloth, one that only appeared from the back of the airing cupboard on special occasions, and spread it carefully over the table. Immediately the atmosphere in the room became special, quiet, an occasion. With a fresh tea-towel she carefully polished the cutlery, each knife, each fork, each spoon.

Suddenly Richard called out. 'Mum! Lady's been sick!'

'What?' Mrs Hart went to the door of the kitchen. 'What?!'

'It's Lady. Eugh. It's Lady. She's been sick. There's some on the board!'

Mrs Hart thrust the knife and peeled sprout she was holding into the saucepan with the other waiting sprouts and went into the living room.

'Did you give her one of your chocolates?' she asked.

'No! I haven't opened them.' He and Carol were always given a Selection Box of chocolates at Christmas. 'I'm not going to waste a bar of fudge on Lady, even if she wins the game. Which she won't.'

Mrs Hart looked at Carol who was peering into the living room. 'Did she eat some of yours?'

'No!'

'Who took her out this morning? Did she eat something then?'

'No,' said Richard. 'She was only out two minutes.'

Their mother groaned. 'Oh no.'

'What? Is she ill?' Richard cried.

'What is it?' Carol looked at her mother's face.

'Get a sheet.'

'Is she dying?' Richard shrieked.

'No. No! Be quick. A sheet. She needs somewhere quiet.'

'What's wrong with her?'

'She's having puppies.'

'Is she?' Richard laughed. 'Puppies?'

'Where's your father?'

'Which sheet?' asked Carol.

'Any sheet. Something clean for her to lie on.'

Richard dashed out of the room. There was a clatter. He came back, dragging the table cloth.

Mrs Hart who was kneeling beside Lady, gently feeling Lady's belly, reached behind her to take it.

'The tablecloth!' Carol shouted.

'Not the tablecloth,' Mrs Hart moaned. 'Where's your father? She's his dog.'

'She's my dog,' Richard said.

Carol ran upstairs to the bathroom and hauled a sheet from the airing cupboard. Two nighties floated out into the bath, and she hesitated, but left them there and ran back down. Together she and her mother eased Lady onto the sheet. 'Richard, get her basket,' Mrs Hart called. With difficulty they lifted her up.

'There! There!' With her chin Mrs Hart indicated to Richard the far corner by the television and as he dropped the basket, they slid Lady onto the faded red cushion. She looked up at them with big eyes and Mrs Hart bent down and stroked her head.

There was the sound of a key in the lock. 'I've got the milk!' Mr Hart called. 'It's a Christmas miracle.'

'At last! Frank! In here!' Mrs Hart called. 'Your dad can take over now.'

'What's wrong? What's burning?' Mr Hart stood in the hall, unbuttoning his mac.

'Lady's having puppies!' Richard called.

'Now? Now?' Mr Hart hurried into the room.

'What do you mean what's burning?' Mrs Hart rose to her feet. 'Oh my god. What's burning?'

A wisp of smoke floated into the living room.

Carol threw a glance around the room. 'Well, it's not the Christmas tree.'

'It's the pudding!' Mrs Hart ran into the kitchen. 'And the sprouts,' she wailed. 'Who lit the gas under the sprouts?'

The smell of burning was stronger.

'Does this mean we shan't have sprouts?' Richard whispered gleefully.

'I love sprouts,' Carol said sadly.

Mr Hart was crouched beside Lady, feeling her belly. Lady shivered.

There was a crash from the kitchen. 'Right!' shouted Mrs Hart. 'There goes the chicken! Frank! Frank!'

'Go and help your mother,' Mr Hart muttered. 'I can't leave Lady.'

Carol leaped to her feet and disappeared into the kitchen.

'Shall I go?' Richard murmured unenthusiastically.

'You stay here with me. I shall need a hand with this.'

'OK,' Richard said weakly. He wiped the small mess from the Monopoly board with his hanky. There was a stain. He would never forget how it got there, he told himself.

'We've got to move Lady out to the shed,' his dad said. 'She needs peace and quiet.' Together they slowly lifted the basket. Lady looked out mournfully. 'It's the arrival of the Magi,' Mr Hart announced as they moved majestically into the hall.

'You're not coming through the kitchen,' Mrs Hart spoke sharply, kneeling on the floor wiping away great semi-circles of grease. 'But you can leave the gold at the door.' She looked up and gave them a wan smile.

Carol stepped carefully over a half-roasted potato. 'I'll open the French windows,' she said.

'You know the dinner's ruined, don't you?' Carol murmured to her dad.

'Oh dear,' he said. 'I thought this was all going to happen next week.' He and Richard moved slowly across the wet grass to the shed, and Mr Hart manoeuvred open the shed door. Gently they set down the basket and lowered Lady, still in the sheet, into her special box.

'Will she be all right?' James asked, stepping back, looking down at Lady circling in her box, getting comfortable.

'She'll be fine,' Mr Hart said. 'Whereas I shall certainly not be in your mother's good books for the rest of the day, at least. You'd better go and tell her that I may be some time. Lady's going to want me close at hand, I think.'

Richard wanted to run round to Malcolm's house and watch anything on telly. He wanted to go upstairs and read a sensible book. Anything but go into the kitchen and tell his mum that dad was going to be a long while. He dragged his way back through the French windows, took as long as he could wiping his feet on the little rag rug, and then headed to the kitchen. Where his mum and Carol were laughing. 'Why are you laughing?'

They carried on giggling.

'Dad says he's got to stay out in the shed for ever with Lady.'

'It won't be for ever, love,' his mum said. 'But it might be a little while. We're laughing, well, because we've got hysterics, really, and also because Christmas dinner is not going to happen as we thought. We are going to have a picnic in the living room.'

'A picnic?'

'With chicken sandwiches and some tinned apricots and evaporated milk.' I thought the chicken fell on the floor,' Richard said suspiciously.

'We have taken off the skin,' his mum said. He realised they were buttering bread. 'We'll take a plate to your dad in the shed.'

'Will we still have crackers?' Richard asked.

'Of course.'

'All right then,' Richard said.

'Come and help me straighten the table cloth on the floor,' Carol said.

'And then I'll open the box of crackers,' Richard said.

There was a shout from the shed. Mrs Hart opened the back door. 'The first one has come,' Mr Hart called. 'All's well.'

'I'll bring you out a sandwich and a bottle of Bass,' Mrs Hart replied.

'And don't forget the mistletoe,' he said.

'Don't push it,' Mrs Hart said.

ACKNOWLEDGMENTS

My thanks go to the following:

Maureen Hanscomb for her encouragement, patience and careful suggestions. To Sue Katz for being a lifeline during lockdown with our daily Zoom writing sessions, and who provided wonderful critical commentary as well as introducing me to the notion of the 100-word story. Never forgetting John Petherbridge who had faith in me all those years ago in the class at City Lit in London. And to my agent Annette Green for continuing to have faith.

To all the mods in Chelmsford who made life in the Sixties so exciting and so much fun, especially at Christmas, in particular to Christine Rand whose stalwart friendship made it all possible.

To Christine Wilkinson for the wonderful cover design.

And as ever, my greatest thanks to Caroline Spry, for her love, confidence and encouragement, without which none of this would get past the dreaming stage.

ABOUT THE AUTHOR

Elizabeth Woodcraft was born and grew up in Chelmsford. She was a mod at 13 and took her suede coat to Birmingham University. She became a teacher and taught in Leicester and Tours in France. She then moved to London where she worked for Women's Aid, the organisation which supports women who suffer domestic violence. Her experiences there led her to become a barrister.

As well as her books about the Sixties, Elizabeth Woodcraft has published two crime novels, featuring barrister Frankie Richmond – Good Bad Woman and Babyface. Good Bad Woman was shortlisted for the John Creasey Award for Best First Crime Novel, and in the US won the Lambda Literary Award.

She lives in London with her partner.

Contact her on www.elizabethwoodcraft.com
Follow her on Twitter @lizwoodcraft

Printed in Great Britain
by Amazon

14012447R00103